All Jack Preston has ever wanted is freedom: from his father's oppressive political reign, from his mother's dying memory, from his own guilt in the part he's played to get George Preston to the top. When an assassination attempt is made on his father's life, Jack is thrown into a dangerous game of lies and espionage, and as his whole world destabilizes, he finds himself turning to the most unlikely person for help.

Alex—the assassin who started it all; the man whose face haunts Jack's dreams—becomes his only ally. As they come together to fight a bigger enemy, Jack's attraction becomes a risk too large to take and too powerful not to. Will falling in love with a dangerous killer play right into his enemy's hands? Or will Alex risk everything to protect the son of the man he was sent to murder? Loyalties will be tested and sacrifices made, but Jack will learn that some things are truly worth fighting for.

Published by
NineStar Press
PO Box 91792
Albuquerque, New Mexico, 87199
www.ninestarpress.com

Warning: This book contains sexually explicit content which is only suitable for mature readers.

Print ISBN #978-1-911153-67-2
Cover Art by Natasha Snow
Edited by Lisa Cox

DEFIANT
LOYALTIES

Elizabeth Wilde

Chapter One

As a kid, he'd looked for hours out of this window right here.

This same mahogany window seat. This same view of the park. This same flower box with its pink carnations.

At twenty-nine, the only thing that's changed to him is the vista of the city, a skyline that alters almost monthly now, but he's usually a part of it, not surveying from the fourth floor of a fortress. He thinks, idly, that his own apartment is somewhere off in this direction, a few miles south across the river.

"Are you even listening to me?"

Jack cringes. "Sure, Dad, always listening."

"This is *my* roof, you hear me?" His dad feels it's appropriate to point to the actual roof to absolutely hammer home the point. "And while you're here, you behave, you got that?"

It's always questions with his father; Jack's been here less than a day and he'd forgotten what it was like to be at constant war with rhetoric.

"Yeah, I got it," he says dryly. "No fucking guys in your townhouse."

George Preston kept his head through the cold war and the Broneburg city riots, but now he colors that certain, specific shade of red that makes Jack viciously pleased.

His dad paces in the confines of the study like a dangerous animal caged, and all Jack can think is *Getting a little gray, there, Dad* with the patchy light spilling in, catching the silver in his dark hair.

"You're here by my good graces—"

Jack scoffs. "I'm here for photographs and clickbait. I'm here because I got Mom's looks and your height and am, unfortunately, your only kid to parade around when re-election rolls up."

He's here because he'd promised her, years and years ago while she faded away on the satin sheets, that he'd never abandon his father.

"Well, we're clear on that, at least," George drawls, displaying his uncanny skill of switching out one emotion for another as quickly as blinking. His smile is cool when it appears, papering over the cracks of his moment of weakness. He's always looked out of place amongst the warmth of this house, the walnut woods and the heavy drapes, pruning his expressions for those who don't know him well enough to see the calculating glint in his snake eyes. "Show me up and you'll regret it, Jack."

"Wouldn't dream of it, Dad."

"Like hell you wouldn't."

"I'm hardly a delinquent," Jack fires back. "We manage to stay out of each other's way most of the time, and you never hear a peep out of me."

"Do you know how much I had to pay out to keep your little affair with Senator Leigh's son out of the press?"

"Yes, because in eight years you have *never* let me forget it."

"Photographs on my desk at six AM is one hell of a way to find out your child is a—"

"Do we have to have this discussion every time I come here?"

"We do when I have to fend off the question *when's that son of yours gonna settle down and have a family* every Goddamn time you get brought up."

Under his breath but still loud enough to hear, Jack mutters, "Couldn't afford to have a fucking family in this city."

"Maybe if you got a real job instead of that crap you paint, started getting to know some upstanding folk—"

"I could be *just* like my father," he snaps.

And because they're alike in the pettiest ways only, it's his dad's turn to mutter under his breath, "And what an improvement that'd be."

There's little more that needs to be said. George slips on a coat and out the study door, telling him, "I'll be at the lodge if anyone asks." Jack paces a while, following his father's groove in the carpet and feeling twitchy and unsatisfied, a vaguely displaced energy thrumming in him.

He grabs his own jacket, keys, wallet, phone, and slams the front door with a rattle loud enough to upset the neighbors.

It's spring in the city.

The weather soaks everything and cuts the rain with high-voltage winds, unnaturally volatile for Broneburg at any time of the year but the turn of summer especially. The clouds roll over, patching the cornflower sky in whites and grays, darker until the rain comes again and then splitting suddenly wide open to let the sun through.

It's indecisive, and Jack kind of likes it—suits his mood, at any rate.

He pulls his jacket tight around him and walks, the bottom of his jeans turning dark with the gloss of sidewalk rain. The neat row of white-and-smokestone townhouses behind him and the gray concrete and wrought-iron fence of the park up ahead.

He takes the path through the park, past the vacant playground, swings swaying in the wind like a haunting. It's nostalgic like every time he comes back uptown, the climbing frame he fell off as a kid a phantom ache in his back and the thoroughfare lined with sugar maples where he skated himself to a broken leg through a pile of autumnal leaves. The street beyond it and the corner spot by the lamppost where Buck Scharber used to fence PowerMac parts and scented candles and stationary out of his pickup; motherboards and little yellow pencils stuffed into overflowing boxes on his truck bed.

The park divides the city, and farther south, the river Wilbec divides it again, three chunks of urban sprawl slowly concentrating wealth and disseminating decay from the top down.

When he was young, shops lit up Broneburg's north-central boulevard. Candy from Yoki's Sweet Factory and then, later, when he was growing out his hair and wearing tacky rainbow belts with silver studs, coffee from Romano's and weed from Shawn's place above the launderette.

He tips his head against the momentarily dry wind and makes quick work of the boulevard now; no launderette, no shops, and Shawn'd need three more jobs and a fucking lottery win before he could afford one of the condos here.

The eighty-four bus comes to a hydraulic stop on the main road up ahead, and Jack jogs the last hundred yards to hop aboard, holding the ceiling rail and swaying with the stop-start motion.

He watches the city contract, pile up on itself, bus turning left at the end of the main intersection and onto Laurel Street where the fast food restaurants start populating the sidewalks. It's raining again, patter sound of it on the metal and like evening outside the way the sky's suddenly an opaque gray.

Laurel Street turns, running parallel with the river, and then after another turn, the bus rolls over the bridge where the wind is the worst, battering rain against the windows, Jack's hand gripping white-knuckled around the rail.

Ten minutes later, he hits the real downtown, clouds breaking up as fast as they gathered as he steps off the bus and back into familiar territory.

The South Plaza by day is a medley of open storefronts, food trucks and high street fashion. Lined on both sides of its cobbled street by welcoming cafés and less welcoming bars, dank little alleys spanning off like spider veins. Jack got his first drunken tattoo down one of them—a smudged-looking lizard on his hip that he'd found hilarious at the time, not so much afterwards.

At night, they call it the Moonlight Mile for its mile-long stretch of light and vivacious sound.

He makes a beeline for Sol's bar, feeling damp and still vaguely irritated, the whole bus ride not enough to shake the uncomfortable lump sitting in his stomach. The sense of being at odds with himself is miserably familiar; every day, month, year he gets itchier in his own skin.

It's warm like a blast furnace when he opens the heavy front door to Sol's and he weaves around the cramped little tables, ducking the trinkets hanging from the ceiling: pots, beads, a fucking ancient bicycle of all things.

"Wow." Sol stops wiping down a glass to roll up a crisp, white shirt-cuff and check her watch from behind the bar. He's surprised she can make it out under the faint lighting, against the sleeve of dark tattoos winding up her arm. "You lasted six hours."

Jack hops a barstool, elbow holding up his slump against the counter. "I'm going back, don't get smug."

She measures him with a look, cocking a dark eyebrow. "That bad, huh?"

"I sorta…" He huffs a laugh. "Forgot. What he was like."

"Come on, he's on the news enough."

"I make a point to switch channels."

"Good choice. The other night he was talking about plans for the next batch of luxury high-rises," Sol says flatly, flipping a glass and filling it with beer from the tap. She puts it down in front of him, waving him away when he reaches for his wallet. "Like *that's* what we need."

"Uptown is weird, Sol," he tells her, pushing his finger through the condensation mottling his glass. "Like a time warp, only the cars are getting bigger."

"Your daddy's playground, honey. Half his congressional staff live on that street now."

Jack grins. "And Mrs. Mosley, she still lives there."

Sol brightens at that. "Aww, really? Man, that old broad has got some gold stashed somewhere."

"She'd have to, wouldn't she? Although why she'd wanna live amongst the vipers, I don't know." He scrubs his hand through his hair with a groan. "I gotta get this bitterness out of my system or I'm not gonna survive this."

"It's five weeks, it'll pass in no time, and then you can go back to being a crappy artist in a studio apartment on the wrong side of the tracks."

"Crappy," he deadpans.

"Unappreciated in your time," Sol corrects. "And single."

"Could be less than five weeks," Jack points out. "I'm not good at keeping my mouth shut around him."

"Doesn't he need his loyal, six-two babe of a son on his arm to sway the lady and youth voters, though?" Sol asks, genuinely curious, and then adds spitefully, "To distract everyone from the fact he's the *devil*?"

"Don't underestimate how much he resents me."

"Then fuck it up. Go to town on that son of a bitch."

Jack sighs, long-suffering. "You know I can't—"

"I get it, you promised your mom, but she's been gone nineteen years, Jack, and I don't think she'd be all that hot about the guy your father turned into."

He drains half his beer in a few gulps, that festering knot in his stomach churning. "Well, we'll never know, will we?"

It's easy enough to lean on the promise he made to his mom, that unbreakable death-bed vow, but Jack agrees: his mom would've hated George Preston and everything he took a stand for in the years following her death. He doesn't know what keeps drawing him into this charade, some grasp for a connection maybe, to keep the fraying thread of family alive for just a bit longer. His dad's seat in office is pretty much a slam dunk, and Jack's presence is insurance at best, George the kind of man who lets no stone go unturned when he has a goal in mind, and so it's on Jack, truly, why the hell he puts up with it.

"Charles Hampton was acquitted today on charges of drug trafficking, extortion, the laundering of millions of dollars—"

"Fucking acquitted?" Sol snaps, head tipped back toward the TV bracketed on the wall. "I want the number of this guy's lawyer. I got some way overdue parking tickets that I could use a hand with."

"Meanwhile, the investigation on Mason Lorde continues, but could this shocking acquittal be a sign of things to come?"

"Wait, *acquitted*?" Jack asks, Sol nodding. "Not even reduced sentence—actually let off scot-free?"

"Yup."

He's surprised, and he's not even sure why, looking into Charles Hampton's insincere face as he gives a speech on the steps of the court house.

"He got off, huh?"

Jack turns into the booming voice behind him, vaguely gesturing to Shawn in greeting.

Shawn pulls the trucker cap off his huge bald head and takes a seat on the stool beside Jack. Sol pulls him a beer, again waving off the payment.

"I thought his head might roll," Shawn goes on, taking her hand for a brief second.

Jack huffs a laugh. "You always say that."

"And I'm wrong a lot lately."

"Lemme guess," Sol drawls. "If you'd been prosecuting, you'd have taken them all to the cleaners."

"Damn straight I would."

"I bet everyone who studied law says that," Jack quips.

"I wouldn't know." Shawn grins. "I can't remember half of law school."

He smells damp and diesely from his work up at the factory, and Jack mourns Shawn's failed law career, incorruptible bloodhound that he is. Sol, too; there's a diploma tucked away amongst the old black-and-white Eric Clapton and Elmore James photographs on the back wall of the bar: Ramona Solomon who graduated catering with honors. She makes a reasonable living here, despite ongoing battles with brewers and landlords, but her oldest passions stay unsatisfied.

Jack looks at them sometimes, the people he's known and loved all his life, and knows this isn't what any of them dreamed of when they were younger.

He knows he's feeling overly sentimental and intensely nostalgic, the long days to come staying in his childhood home filling him with a kind of morbid indulgence. He wishes he could shake it, but he's reactive by nature, emotions always simmering away somewhere under the surface; easy with affection and quick to rile.

"I gotta pull my head out of my ass," he mutters, earning twin odd looks.

Sol exercises her eyebrow at him again. "Excuse me?"

"Suck it up," he explains, slapping a hand on the bar top. "Quit being such a baby."

"That's the spirit," Shawn toasts. "How are things at the high castle?"

"They're gonna be awesome, I'm gonna get through it, I'm *not* gonna complain"—Sol scoffs—"and Sol's gonna shut her big yap."

"Sounds pretty farfetched to me." Sol smirks.

Shawn mutters into his drink, "Especially that last part," and Sol pretends to preen, tossing her dark hair.

Jack watches them laugh and talk a while, content to sit in his own head, pretending his resolution is worth a damn.

Life here is both easy and difficult; creating commission artwork under a false name for just enough money to get by—and often less than that—and trying to keep a low profile at all times to avoid any kind of family scandal. Most of the time he's glad for it, happy to take his lot over the money and prestige his father's path laid out for him, the townhouse with its oppressive atmosphere that smothers like a wet blanket and leaves him cold and tense. But he gets frustrated at himself for the blurred line he can't seem to completely settle on one side of, living a kind of double life that's way less interesting than the term sounds.

For each of us going home must be like trying to render an account—he read that in a book, once, and it stuck.

Every so often Jack's account needs settling up, and he pays his dues with a dozen little self-delusions and personal sacrifices, gritting his teeth the whole time and reminded of all the ways he isn't a whole person.

Something will break. The inevitability of it sits at odd angles like a shadow, just out of sight and imminently looming, a dark amassment of unknown consequence.

Chapter Two

By the time he steps off the eighty-four bus, it's nine PM and the sun is down.

The streets are empty, people tucked up inside away from the wind, faint, sleepy lights glowing out from behind the window curtains.

The rain has long stopped, and when he looks up at the darkening sky, low clouds blow over and over like smoke billows as quickly as he can walk under them.

Feels like a storm, he thinks idly, passing back through the thoroughfare that looks more like the setting of a horror movie by dark: golden sugar maples turned black and imposing, swaying to a sound like waves at sea.

It's just one of those strange nights, swollen with murky promise, and Jack welcomes the odd satisfaction it gives him, the little shiver under his skin that speaks to his pen hand. Upheaval is good for one thing at least, makes his brain churn out concepts and colors he itches to put to paper.

Maybe tonight he will. He has a commission on the books, something nice and subversive for a guy out in the sticks running an alternative porn racket from his deceased parents' old pig farm. If Jack's father only knew—

He unlocks the door to the townhouse, stepping into the pitch-black hall, and because he's still a little tipsy it takes a few seconds to realize there's anything weird about that.

Or not. There might not be. His father may well still be at the lodge, housekeeper finished and left hours ago. The place is most likely empty, and he gets a second to muse *could've brought some guy home to fuck after all* before the thought snuffs out with the sound of the creaking upstairs floorboards.

"Dad?" Nothing, not a sound, and he tries again, standing at the bottom of the stairs and shouting upward, "Dad, you home?"

It's a little eerie how his voice echoes.

These old townhouses are hollow and creaky, and God knows he freaked out enough about it when he was a kid, but it doesn't stop the little drop of cold rippling in his stomach. The subtly off feeling that there's something wrong.

Jack climbs most of the way up the staircase to peer down the hall. It's all dark except for a single strip of light seeping out from the crack underneath his father's study door.

Oh. Another thing he'd forgotten all about.

He knocks gently. "Dad?" But he knows from experience he isn't going to get an answer.

Jack clicks the door open, hit by the familiar sight of his dad passed out over his desktop, half-empty bottle of Old Fitzgerald at his elbow. The curtains blow in from the open window, and the desk lamp glows, and the whole room smells like the bar Jack left half an hour ago.

He scrubs a hand over his face, scratching across his late stubble.

"I'm not coming over there," he tells his dad's slumped body. "I'm not doing it."

George, predictably, says nothing.

"You're gonna fuck up your back, you know that?" He doesn't have a clue why he waits for a reply, but he does, leaving an appropriate amount of silence before going on. "Fuck up your back like you've fucked up everything else."

Jack takes a couple of steps into the room, folding his arms tight over his chest, hesitating even though he knows he is, in fact, going to go over there. If nothing else, just to turn off the light.

"You're a mess," he says, harder than he means it to come out. "What am I even doing here?"

He moves the whiskey to a side cabinet, scoops up some scattered papers and stacks them neatly in the letter tray, turns the desk light off and feels the searing heat burning off it.

"Coulda set fire to the whole place, you idiot," he chastises, even though he knows that's probably not true; he just wants to say it, get in these petty little digs while his dad can't answer back for once.

Jack lets his eyes adjust to the dark, fixed on his father's back steadily rising and falling.

It's not like he'd thank you for waking him up, is what he tells himself. And then: *Why the hell do you even care?* Which is also a really good point.

He scrubs his hand over his face again, a sound of frustration trying to climb its way out of his throat, and in his moment of partial blindness, the floor by the open window *creaks*.

Curtains shifting—window wide open—

Jack's chest hollows out, all the air in his lungs seemingly vanished. A detachedness comes over him, a kind of anesthetizing cold clutching at his limbs until he's not in control of them anymore, until he's slowly turning around to face the moonlight spilling in from the *wide-open fucking window*.

An instinct to move brutally kicks in, making him lurch forward toward the door, but he only makes it halfway, a black figure appearing out of his peripheral blind spot like his worst Goddamn nightmare.

It tackles him, and he can't stop the momentum throwing him sideways.

Jack's body collides with a bookshelf, another body into him, and he lashes out frantically with an elbow and as much of his unfocused weight as he can put behind it, connecting with something solid: an actual living, breathing person trying to fucking attack him in his dad's study.

A shockingly real hand grips the back of his jacket, and he

opens his mouth to shout out—for what good it'd do with his father passed out drunk—but a foot hooks around his calf and trips him, sending him falling to his knees on the carpet with his arm twisted up against his back.

The incapacitation knocks a wild panic loose in him, an urgent fight-or-flight reflex, and he's no stranger to a brawl, to fighting dirty when he has to. Riding the wave of adrenaline, Jack throws his head back into a sternum hard enough to wind.

His attacker staggers back, heaving a gasp in the silence—male, definitely male—and Jack clambers to his feet. This is the part where he's supposed to run, find a safe place to call the cops, but his dad—Jack senselessly hesitates for the smallest moment it takes for his attacker to yank him off balance, spin him face-to-face.

This guy is absolutely not here to rob them, Jack very quickly processes, and then a fist comes at him for his crime of being too slow.

Jack barely avoids it, catching the tail-end of some seriously bruising force against the forearm he throws up to block, power behind the punch honed and practiced.

He uses the split-second unbalance to grip the guy's wrist and grapple with him, trying to catch the other one. Jack's bigger, he realizes, got height and bulk on his opponent, and he uses it to force him back with a crack against the wall beside the door—kicked shut, he notices with a sickening shudder.

"Who the hell are you?" Jack rasps, reeling and unthinking, and the man he's got pinned freezes for a blurry second before he strikes out with another fist to Jack's stomach, sending him doubling over and wheezing.

Another hit connects with his cheekbone and rattles his brain, and he surges up into it, throwing a furious punch of his own and feeling the bite of teeth in his knuckles as he splits open a lip.

It's like a switch flipped; they crash together, dirty jabs and then schoolyard grappling, and all the while Jack's ears ring, and his hazy vision starts to register blood slick from a full bottom lip, bright eyes and dark eyelashes.

Jack sinks a fist deep into hair that's longer on top and *yanks* back, hard as he can.

It's like a gut-punch, suckered low and delivered with uncomfortable sharpness, when he realizes what he's trying to do is get a good long look at the bastard.

Dressed in black tactical gear, hair dark, skin pale, eyes some shade of green in the waxy moonlight. He's a few inches shorter than Jack, slimmer, and fucking beautiful like a dream, caught here by Jack's hand in this utterly surreal moment.

His fingers curl against Jack's sides and his mouth parts for breath, but other than that, he's shocked still, the blunt exposure seemingly freezing him.

Jack's voice cracks: "Who are you?"

He shouldn't have let himself look, he shouldn't have—the guy takes advantage of the slip, headbutting Jack and cracking his vision into comet trails.

They scuffle briefly, ending with Jack slammed on his back with the shadow of a body looming over him, barely visible with his head still full of firecrackers.

Unmistakable, though, even in the chaos, is the swift metallic click of a handgun and the bite of a cold barrel into the side of Jack's face.

He's gonna fucking die. This is it, the part where his life flashes before his eyes, but all he can get his brain to cough up is the face of the son of a bitch who's about to end him; stalled, stalled and burned there forever in his very last moments, and when they figure out how to look through the eyes of a dead man this is what they'll see. The disquieting elegance of a cold-blooded killer.

And then—nothing.

Jack blinks back the sparking synapses behind his eyes, view clearing until the man comes back into focus, hunched down with the gun trained.

His mouth is a tight line and his eyes wide and sharp, expression all lethal intention even as he doesn't pull the trigger. He's so still he's almost inhuman, on and on with that damn gun on Jack, silent waiting twisting him up tighter and tighter until he's starting to tremble and yet—maybe he's lost his fucking mind because he doesn't think, in his gut, that the guy is going to shoot him.

And Jack's gut is clearly running the show right now because he's right.

The man stands in one fluid movement, Jack holding his breath at the quiet unfurling of that body over him. He holds the gun out to his side, metal reflecting up the eddies of moonlight, and pins Jack down with the look on his face.

"I'm sorry about this," he says, hoarse like he hasn't used his voice in a while, and Jack's so shocked by the sound of it, the rough authenticity of it, he almost doesn't see the man's hands deftly screwing a suppressor onto his weapon.

The weapon now pointing at Jack's unconscious father.

"No no no—"

That's him, that's Jack begging right now, shuffling up to his elbows on the floor where he can't do a damn thing but watch.

Except he can, he can do *something*.

"No!"

Jack pushes himself up to sitting, gripping the man's belt and pulling down every bit of his weight to drag him away, down, *anything*; fingers desperately scrabbling for purchase against the slippery nylon of the gear.

The man turns, and Jack narrowly avoids a kick to the face, curling a hand into the front of the belt now, a metal clasp cutting into the joints of his fingers, and he pulls and pulls until he can secure the killer's gun hand in his own much larger one. The guy falls to his knees on the carpet, thighs bracketing Jack's hips, and

Jack's neck bent back to keep him in his eye-line.

They grapple close-quarters, too little space to wind up any hits, and Jack catches both the man's wrists and yanks them outwards from his sides, the gun as far away from them both as he can get it.

Jack's opened him right up, he realizes. Opened him up right here in Jack's lap on his dad's study floor. The man's chest heaves, his face turned down, and the rapid rise and fall of his stomach keenly felt against Jack's ribs, every hard breath hitting Jack's mouth and pulling into his own dizzy lungs.

The guy tries to take his hands back but Jack holds tight and the effect is obscene, rocking them together, as messed up as Jack's ever felt in his whole damn life. Quick twin pulses throb against Jack's thumbs, and his own heart hammers under his ribcage, and the attacker wets his split bottom lip, looking immediately startled at the reactive hitch of Jack's breath.

His whole nervous system flaring into a heat whirlwind, Jack blindly, compulsively, slides his thumbs over and over the soft underside veins of the man's wrists, feels the slackening of the gun hand through the tendons there.

"Who are you?" Jack asks for a third time; who or *what, where the* fuck *did you come from? Why are you doing this?*

The man's throat looks so appealingly slick with sweat in this silvery light as it bobs on a swallow and yeah, Jack's truly out of his mind, senses scattered to the moonlight. He's scared, fuck, so scared it's inside him, writhing like a thing on a live wire, and this person in his lap is looking at him with a slowly explicit horror, *letting* Jack touch him like this—

They startle apart at the sound of his dad groaning, shifting, and then Jack's looking up at the world from flat on his back, his head *throbbing*, the ceiling swimming, darkening, fading, fading.

Chapter Three

He presses his fingertips underneath the tacky wound at his temple, down to the purpling bruise on his cheek.

Leftovers, unassailable proofs or—or disturbing keepsakes. Of the most surreal damn moment of his life, all of it still like a fever dream borne from the part of his brain where he's still a teenager stuffed full on action movies and raging hormones.

Jack stares at his reflection, filled with the odd sensation that he hardly recognizes the person looking back at him. It's only a semi-ridiculous way to feel, the injuries really inconsequential to look at, but they root deeper in him somehow, call his whole structure into question.

He could've died. Jack could've died, his father could've died, and he'd almost—what? What had he almost done? Let his fascination for the sinister grip him in dire straits at the very least. He can still taste the blood in his mouth, has a tender cut on the soft inside of his cheek—and if he dares to shut his eyes, Jack can see gunmetal and green.

The knock on his bedroom door puts the thoughts to temporary rest, his dad waltzing in without waiting for permission enough to irritate him in that distracting, familiar way.

But George is uncharacteristically thoughtful, coming to a stop behind Jack and studying him in the mirror for a solid thirty seconds before Jack snaps, "What?"

His dad tips his chin. "How is it?"

"Got a headache, but I'll live."

"I, uh," his father starts, stops; God, Jack's never seen him so unsure of himself. "I wanted to say thanks, for, y'know."

"Saving your life?"

He gets a dry look for that. "Yeah, that."

"Don't mention it."

"Good thing I tried to make you a marine, huh?" Jack raises an eyebrow at his father's reflection, and when George goes on, it's a gentle kind of ribbing instead of the usual scathing indictment. "Maybe if you'd stuck it out, you coulda caught the bastard."

Jack nods, drawling, "Yeah, all right, Dad, think that's thanks enough for today."

There's a soft pause, and then, "I've upped security."

"Cops?"

"No, contractors."

"Private military contractors?" Jack turns around. "Where are the police?"

"I haven't called them."

"Yet, or?"

His dad huffs, inexplicably impatient now. "I don't want the police involved."

"Someone—" Jack has to stop a second, scrunching his face up. "Someone tried to *kill* you last night. Someone who was carrying what I'm pretty sure was a sound-suppressed, military-grade handgun."

"You don't get to be congressman for as long as I have without a few attempts on your life. It was bound to happen eventually."

"*What*? Are you—are you kidding me?" Jack's voice is going high-pitched; he can't help it. "I think most people in office go their whole lives without one real assassination attempt to their name. This isn't Stalin's Russia, Dad, it's a crappy city in the twenty-first century Midwest."

George hand-waves him off. "I said no police; this discussion is over. They're already here. The team leader wants to talk to you—she needs a description of the guy."

All the commotion downstairs and Jack had assumed it was the police. He frowns, buying himself some time to compose his face before he can say, "I can't help her. His face was covered."

His dad swears under his breath, "Fuck." And then, "Go talk to her anyway. They're changing the locks, installing a new alarm system, all that crap."

How untouchable did his father think he was before now? Jack stares after his retreating figure, struck dumb by his arrogance. In all the years Jack's lived, visited and stayed here, he's never once had to deal with the rusty-looking but definitely present door alarm. It never even struck him as dangerous until right this minute, but his dad is calculating to the extreme, four steps ahead of everyone else's thought processes, and the oversight is jarring.

He shakes himself out of it, pulls on a sweater against the chill of the house, and heads out into the hall.

The study sits pretty at the other end, and he aches for just a still second, shot through with the stark physical sense of his injuries.

I'm sorry about this—that's what the assassin had said.

Fucking weird, everything about this. His head's crammed full with it, still tender and sorely reeling. Every heavy step he takes down the stairs doesn't make it any more real.

The team leader is in the dining room, blueprint plans of the house spread out across the table. She looks up when he enters, standing straight and offering her hand.

"Mr. Preston."

Her voice is smooth and low and she's almost a whole foot shorter than him, slender palm in his own with a ruthless handshake. "Call me Jack, please."

She smiles lopsidedly, laugh lines deep around her hazel eyes. "Jack. You can call me Regina."

"Nice to meet you, uh." He rubs the back of his neck. "This is all a little sudden, so pardon my greenness."

"You served in the Infantry for a year," she says slyly. "You're not that green."

"A *long* time ago. It's a little different from having a killer roll up and beat the crap out of you."

"You held your own. It's more than most."

He huffs a laugh. "Yeah, well, it'd be nice to know why I had to."

"Well," Regina says slowly, "it's not my job to investigate this—it's my job to protect you and your father." She hands him a ring with two keys and a folded scrap of paper. "Front door, back door. Alarm code is written down—memorize and destroy it. When you plan to leave the house, tell me or one of my guys, and we'll arrange an escort. On that piece of paper there's also a contact number to be used under any circumstance you feel in danger. Put it in your phone as something innocuous, and don't be afraid to call it. That's why we're here."

"An escort?"

"It's something your father specifically requested," she tells him. "Obviously, I can't force my guys on you, but at minimum a heads-up when you come and go is important."

"Right, so no escort but probably a tail?"

Regina gives him that smile again. "I'm just doing my job."

Jack nods. "Yeah, I know." He pockets the keys and the paper. "So how's this work—guards on every door? Snipers on the rooftops?"

"Landmines on the perimeter," she adds dryly.

Jack laughs. "Obviously."

"There'll be two guys posted on each of your outside doors and a surveillance team on the house at all times. Your father has a personal guard; I'd ask if you wanted one, but..." She trails off, and he grins. "I'll be either here, in the van, or reachable on that number."

"Got it."

"You got a pretty good look at him, right?"

"His face was covered," he repeats, sounding too tinny and automatic to his own ears. "The lights were all out, and he was dressed in dark gear."

"Height, build?"

"Maybe five-ten, five-eleven?" Jack tells her, and then downright fucking *lies:* "Hard to tell what build in the gear." Because what the hell else is he gonna do? Tell her the exact feeling of his body pressed against Jack's, the curve of his spine arched in Jack's lap, and the exhilarating rush of his blood pumping under Jack's thumbs? "Sorry I can't be more help."

"No, that's fine. It's not like I was expecting a facial composite or anything."

No, but Jack could probably give her one. Why he doesn't do just that, well—he doesn't know. The evident shame written all over his face, maybe.

I'm sorry about this.

He clears his throat hard. It's not like they'd catch the guy anyway. He's probably long gone by now, and Jack's gut tells him that he's not some lone madman out to sate a thirst. If there's another attempt on George Preston's life, it's probably not going to come from the same person.

"It's gotta be a group, right?" he asks her—to clarify, to settle some of his guilt.

"I'd hate to say anything for certain without evidence, but most likely, yeah. Maybe extremists of some kind? Your father is a politician, after all."

"So this is common?"

She considers it for a moment. "Not common, but it happens."

"Pretty well-stocked extremists."

"What d'you mean?"

"He just, he looked military, his gear, his weapon."

"Everyone has access to high-grade equipment these days. Hell, four years ago, I encountered an animal rights group with a storage unit filled with dozens of three-thousand-dollar M320 grenade launchers."

"Whoa, what the hell were they gonna do with those?"

"The whys aren't my department, but I'm guessing it was seriously blow some shit up."

"Naturally," Jack huffs.

"What are you worried about, Jack?" Regina asks him curiously, and for an insane second, he thinks about actually trying to put this thing he's chewing on into words.

"Nah, it's nothing, just my dad and his knack for pissing people off."

"Well, that's what we're here for—to keep those people out."

Jack thanks her, and when he gets back out into the hall, he spots their new guards milling around in the doorway, one of them installing a new lock and the other smoking a cigarette out on the front path. Both of them huge and imposing, enough to make someone a little wet behind the ears take a pause anyway.

He heads back up to his room with a kind of grim resolve, because weeks with his father was enough of a situation but this— he's fallen down the Goddamn rabbit hole here, twisting like a leaf in this unseasonal wind. Solidity has slipped through his fingers and it's a thing he can't abide, feeling so lost.

He fires up his laptop, secures himself behind a proxy, and starts at the basics: high threat groups inside the USA, their attire, their training, their particular weapon brands, anything to give him a leg up.

Is the guy some fanatic? The swift right hand of some extremist group, anarchists like Jack remembers seeing on TV, fire-bombing the courthouse years and years ago. A mercenary for hire, maybe? PMCs like the ones downstairs working for some opposing congress runner or a scorned lobbyist.

Jack gets precisely nothing for his trouble, and he *knows* he's avoiding the issue that's really bothering him, his fingers itching to run across the keyboard.

The possibility that someone far more official and untouchable might want his father dead.

He steels himself and goes deeper, exercising every trick Shawn ever taught him about the web. He searches WikiLeaks and releases under the Freedom of Information Act, hacked emails from an upstate law firm that deals with anonymous corporate whistleblowers for huge amounts of cash.

The more he reads, getting sucked into web-hopping over the most tangentially related subjects, the more he feels thickened, slowed right down by a kind of knowing dread. It's not shock—it's way more inevitable than that—but he is surprised, and *surprised* that he's surprised. He's never once so much as googled his father, too afraid, maybe, of what he'd find. Complaining with his friends is one thing, watching his dad make speeches about taxes in front of concerned crowds another, but willingly subjecting himself to the opinions and private truths of strangers is personal, stings by proxy and feels like responsibility.

Jacob Kalhoff vs. United States case seemingly dropped—

Jacob Kalhoff is a name he's heard in the news.

—Kalhoff would like us to think his shady Wall Street days are through, but is the more local J.K Brokerage really a step away or merely the same business under a different label? His successful lobbying for congressional candidate George Preston is well publicized, but should Preston be more careful over who he climbs into bed with?

He reads more about suspect business transactions than he's ever cared to know, but the more personal stuff is the worst.

I can't prove a thing. The bastard got me on some technicality of lying on my resume FIVE YEARS AGO, but he found out about my sexuality, and that was it, I was out on my ass with a newborn to support—

It's not the only one; George Preston's penchant for ruining people's lives running on a small scale as well as a wider one. He reads and reads until it's a psychical impossibility to take in even one more word, and then he slams his laptop shut, hands resting over the lid like he can keep it all inside.

Bribery, dealing with sketchy people, taking favors—it's government games, and his father is the best player he knows. It's naïve at best to be surprised, and yet here he is, staring at the wall and trying to reconcile the truth with what he already thought he knew. They're the same thing, really, but plausible deniability is a comfortable position.

Still, assassination is pretty steep for run-of-the-mill corruption, and so Jack's main question goes woefully unanswered.

Who the hell is trying to kill his father? And—the man set to do the killing, who the hell is he?

Chapter Four

He's going stir crazy.

Trapped in this fucking house, feeling like the damn walls are narrowing every time he looks at them. It's a gilded cage, and Jack's never been very good at confinement.

The clock ticks on and on, seconds into minutes into hours, and all the while Jack becomes snappish and irate and then maudlin in equal turns, staring at the ceiling or plowing through information on his laptop and feeling more and more like someone's watching him because someone usually fucking is.

The day-shift door guards are named Charlie and Joel, and when Jack needs air, the three of them toss a baseball back and forth in the tiny stretch of enclosed front garden, chatting idly about nothing specific.

Joel's wife is a baker, owns a shop way downtown, and sometime midweek, on a day that blurs together with all the rest but is sunnier than most lately, he brings cupcakes and they take lunch on the bench underneath the lounge window.

A brutal gust of wind saws the top off Jack's iced angel wings, and he's had enough, Goddammit; he needs to get out of this fucking place and away from all the eyes so badly he's almost baying for a fight with a bit of icing.

It's how he ends up in the back of a black Mercedes with tinted windows, looking about as conspicuous as a moving target can be, realizing this particular security service isn't that big on subtlety.

That's just typical of his dad, really. Jack wouldn't have expected any less.

"This feels so unnecessary," is what he says, maybe for the dozenth time, and Charlie snorts, maybe also for the dozenth time.

"Rules are rules, kid."

"Really?" Jack deadpans, expensive upholstery creaking under his ass as he shifts to get comfortable. "Kid?"

"Hey, I'm old enough to be your dad."

"Is this your attempt at fatherly bonding, then?"

Charlie laughs. "Hell no."

Charlie's got a prog-rock band and a long-term girlfriend and zero kids and that's exactly the way they like it.

They drift to a stop at the little fountain square just off the east end of the river, and Jack feels more than a little ridiculous walking next to Charlie, a whole four inches on Jack's six-two and at least twice as broad, pristinely dressed in his shirt and tie while Jack's jeans are ripped at the knee and stuffed haphazardly into his boots.

"When I said I wanted a little freedom, an armed escort wasn't what I had in mind," he reiterates, Charlie the only target he's got for his pointless complaints. "In fact this is the exact opposite of freedom."

Charlie waves him off. "Yeah, yeah. So you come here to do your art shit, huh?"

"Not generally, no," Jack tells him. "Little much for me."

What he means is that this is where every art-schooler comes to gain inspiration or insight or whatever, and Jack used to be no different. This part of the city is beautiful and well kept, and under today's sun, the sandy marble of the fountain rather gleams, the water pale and sparkling exactly like water should do in art.

But they all grow weary of it in the end, moving on to the next spot and then the next after that. Now it's crowded with the young and vibrant, people Jack feels a dampened connection to because he was them, once upon a time. Back then, it was the same; him and Shawn and Sol, others too, girlfriends, boyfriends, the wasters and the strays. They'd eat lunch on the surrounding grass under the cherry blossoms or sit on the lip of the fountain with cigarettes by day, cheap vodka by night.

The commemorative bench plaques are a little more rusted—Sydney Munson, died 1981 and lead architect of the Broneburg airport, or Jack's favorite, Mellissa Gyatso, died 1965 and founded the local art college—but he could still superimpose his image on top of this one.

"Then why are we here?" Charlie asks.

Jack flips open his notebook, trying to judge the light.

"Because my dad's stipulation for not pitching a fit about me leaving the Bastille was that I come here and act like a good son."

"By...drawing a fountain?"

"By being recognized amongst happy young people," Jack says dryly. "You'll see."

Charlie looks thoroughly appalled. "Are we gonna get photographed?"

"Lucky for you, no, but me, definitely."

"And you've done this before?"

Jack chooses a bench with a good view of the fountain and the street in the background. "So many times."

Charlie takes a seat at the other end, shaking his head, and Jack feels less resentful toward the whole chaperone issue now that he has the sun on the back of his neck and a clean page under his hands.

"We're killing a bunch of fish with one grenade, as my dad likes to put it," he explains. "See that guy over in the Cubs shirt? He works for the Broneburg Review, but more importantly he works for my dad. Tomorrow the Preston family will get a sweet article about how *normal* I am. And my dad gets rid of me for a few hours, which works for everyone's sanity."

Charlie shakes his head. "No wonder you went to art school. This crap is complicated."

"I don't hate politics," Jack says softly. "Just what it does to some people."

Charlie reaches over and shoves him a little, chuckling, "That's real deep, man," and Jack snaps out of it, almost very nearly maudlin again; emotions turning on a dime.

Jack grins at him. "I'm not just a pretty face."

"Prove it, kid—let's see what your fancy degree can do."

He settles into it quite fast, good at channeling the worst of life's unrest into ways he can process them better. His flair for the creative is always better when he's unsettled, and that's only one step behind him being in love. Sol always joked that he was *in love* with chaos, and he's been stubbornly trying to prove her wrong ever since.

With mixed success.

Jack sketches the street a while, rather than the fountain. Tries to put the people to graphite and capture some piece of them there, some little twinkle of life. He adds simple details and checks his watch continuously, preparing to be disturbed.

"Prepare to get recognized," he surreptitiously tells Charlie.

Right on cue, she walks up to Jack: a pretty girl in a cornflower-blue dress and sandals, tossing her long hair and smiling a sweet smile that doesn't really reach her eyes. She's perfectly constructed in every way for the greatest show; the exact kind of girl his dad would want him to marry, Jack thinks.

"Aren't you Jack Preston, George Preston's son?" she asks loudly.

He's done this so many times that his grin comes easy. He

shields his face from the sun with the cup of his hand. "Yeah, that's me. What can I do for you, sweetheart?"

The ridiculous spectacle doesn't last all that long. She fawns a little; he smiles and acts like a gentleman and talks animatedly about his father like he's the best thing to ever happen to Broneburg.

Eventually she asks him, "What are you drawing?"

"The city," he tells her, and it's not a lie. He spins the notebook. "Look how beautiful she is."

Jack sees a kid in a plaid shirt snap a photo of them on a phone from where he's lounging on the grass, and the girl in the cornflower dress tells Jack, a lot more genuine than before, "She really is."

When she's gone, Charlie waits a good, respectable ten minutes before he stretches an arm across the bench-back, his face still a picture of amusement. "Ever consider a career in acting?"

"Shut up," Jack groans quietly, adding clouds to his sketch now, shading them that determined gray that dogs almost every day of this turbulent spring. "People I actually know don't usually get to see me doing this crap in person. They have to wait until the stories come out before they can rip me multiple new ones."

The laugh Charlie's clearly been holding in chokes out of him. "Oh, man, so all that's gonna be in tomorrow's press?"

"Press, local social media. For the people that actually give a crap, anyway."

"How embarrassing for you."

"Oh, God," Jack whispers under his breath. "Another incoming."

A figure in a white T-shirt and Wayfarer sunglasses, baseball cap pulled low over his face, makes a beeline for Jack, and he'd been *really* fucking hoping no one would have any genuine follow-up questions to add to this mad charade. He's good enough at pretending when he knows what to say, but outright bullshitting is just painful.

Charlie sniggers, turning his head away to hide it, and Jack forcibly schools his face into another grin, peering up again with his hand shielding his eyes. "What can I do for you, sir?"

"*Sir?*" the figure drawls, sly twist to his real nice mouth, and Jack heats from his cheeks down, feeling unexpectedly pinned in place. "Just admiring your picture, is all."

"Oh, thank you."

The voice puts him on edge. Nice mouth, good shoulders, slim and just short of tall, and Jack's got a type that looks a lot like this; he's a little taken is all. He wishes the guy would take off his cap and sunglasses so Jack could get a better look at him.

"You selling it?"

Jack huffs a laugh, ripping the piece from the notebook. "Here, take it." He holds the paper out, pulling it back an inch when the guy reaches for it. Sue him, he's taking a chance, hopes he's reading the situation correctly, but Charlie's always here to throw down in case the guy's an oversensitive straight-guy stereotype—and isn't that just a hilarious mental image. "Unless you're paying with your number, that is."

It's cheesy as hell, but Jack delivers it with a wry little grin, and the guy laughs, smile as bright and deadly as the sun. "I was hoping you'd say that."

Deadly—

Jack feels his own smile fall. The drawing's being tugged out of his slack grip, but Jack's mind veers abruptly elsewhere, eyes inexplicably honing in on the guy's hand around a little folded piece of paper.

Despite the heat out here, Jack goes cold.

"Please take it," the guy mutters, nothing like the light, flirtatious tone from before but achingly recognizable now, and Jack's gaze snaps upward to his face, the serious twist of his too-fucking-familiar mouth.

The voice is the same weight and shape as the contrary apology in the dark, a grim specter that won't stop haunting Jack.

Please. I'm Sorry.

The folded piece of paper is pushed into his open palm, rough fingertips pressing there for a heart-stopping second, and then Jack's staring up at the water fanning out of the top of the fountain, enigmatic flirter and Goddamn *assassin* vanished back into the ether like just another revenant of Jack's never-ending fever-dream.

"Looks like that phony little display just got you laid, kid," Charlie says, dry as a bone somewhere beside him, but Jack looks straight ahead, rattled to his core and terrified he's going to betray himself just with the look on his face. "That a gay guy thing? Shit, I mean—am I allowed to ask that? I mean the guy was fucking *smoking* hot; I can totally appreciate—"

"You don't have to do that, Charlie," Jack tells him faintly, crushing the paper in his trembling hand. His foot is tapping, leg jittery; little outward tics of climbing adrenaline. "I'm not offended."

"Ah, um, good," Charlie says awkwardly, and Jack's guiltily thankful for it because it keeps him quiet at least.

He's being stalked? By the same guy who tried to murder his father not five nights ago. Stalked but not outright targeted, it seems, and Jack set himself up for this one, really, going on about local social media and the like, wandering around in the bright light of day because he's a little stir crazy and a lot thoughtless.

Every time he thinks he's come to terms with what's going on, it hits him all over again.

Jack carefully side-eyes Charlie, checking that he's looking in the other direction before he surreptitiously spreads the crumpled bit of paper out on top of his fresh notebook page.

Your research hasn't gone unnoticed. We suggest it ceases immediately.

The *we* stands out before the rest of it—*we* fucking who? But it begins to kick in, the implicit threat. He'd thought he was being careful, untraceable, but obviously he was wrong, and the world of internet espionage is actually not like in the movies. Not only is he being stalked, now he's been threatened, by people who are taking notice of where he is and what he's doing.

He's weighed down with an immobilizing dread, the kind of lethargy that steals away his will to do anything except sit very still and turn what just happened over and over again in his head until he's drained every possibility of all reason. If he stands up, he has the hysterical notion he might be shot dead right in the middle of the grass in front of dozens of people. What a headline that would be—

He can't do this here, though, with the potential for people looking at him, and Jack's will is a mulish, tenacious thing when it wants to be. He brings up a knee to balance his notebook against and puts pencil back to paper.

What comes out of his finely shaking hand is a simple two-dimensional cityscape with a pleasing skyline of shining buildings unevenly stacked like toy blocks. Underneath the ground level he mirrors it, flipping the notebook upside down and sketching the same cityscape but faster, rougher. Shading the buildings and then breaking them, making their edges jagged and ugly and the ground they sit in toxic and dying.

He frantically sets the mirrored skyline on fire and then spreads his unsteady hand over the page, pressing in with his fingertips until the paper dents and starts to crunch up and then it's tearing free of the notebook spine as he makes a stiff fist.

Calm down, just—

He takes a few deep breaths. The man could be anywhere right now watching him.

"Let's pack up, Charlie," he says quietly, "head back to the house."

"Sure thing." Charlie stands, cracking his back out, and then gives Jack a sly look. "You got your phone number?"

Jack manages a smile. "Could you maybe not let that get back to my dad? Kinda pisses him off."

Charlie raises his eyebrows. "Seriously? It's the twenty-first century, man."

"Yeah, try tellin' my dad that."

"Hey, I got you, don't worry about it."

"Appreciate it."

They set off back across the square, and yeah, Jack does feel a little sturdier. Because what it really comes down to is this: all he needs to do is what the note told him, heed the warning, and that's all. He doesn't need to overanalyze this to death, just stop being a stubborn bastard for once in his life and do as he's told.

Actually, what Jack *should have* done is fucking told Charlie the second he recognized the guy.

And yet somehow, inexplicably, he'd seemingly trusted that Jack wouldn't, and the irony of that is just too much to bear.

Chapter Five

He wakes up slowly, lines of reality blurred, because in his head he's in the lonely darkness in total blissful solitude, but outside of it, he can hear loud voices, sense anger in them.

"What, *what*—" He rolls over onto his back, scrubbing a hand across his numb-feeling face. "The fuck?"

His dad is definitely amongst the din, but Jack realizes the voices aren't meant for him, muffled and coming from the study down the hall.

The quiet dream clings to him, keeping him restful for a few minutes longer while he tries to hold its trickling sensations between his fingers.

He reaches out for his phone on the nightstand, fumbling with it before his hand will properly close; one-thirty in the afternoon, no wonder he's so fucking groggy. Trying to fall asleep at three AM every night with a head ticking over with apprehension, a sense of endless and unspecific waiting, is taking its toll on him.

The voices from the study lower.

And now he's curious.

He rolls out of bed, pulling on a T-shirt and some sweats, and tries to act like he's not snooping, even though he opens his door slow enough to avoid the creak and steps only on the solid floorboards.

Over the last week his father's study has been guarded unfalteringly by Boyce, Regina's biggest guy, but now he's peculiarly gone, and Jack can get close enough for the voices to clarify.

"—up to my ass in it, George, fucking kids tweeting every damn discrepancy in the stories—"

"I won't tell you to keep your voice down again."

Jack shuffles closer as the voice that isn't his father's quietens.

"If they investigate me—"

"They won't."

"I think you underestimate the pressure I'm under here."

"No, I just don't care, because you took my money, Harry. I deal with my own problems, and I'm paying you enough to deal with yours."

A surly silence and then, "How can you be so sure they won't investigate?"

"Because I know some guys."

Harry laughs. "You know some guys, fucking wonderful."

"It is," his father says, slowly, like he's talking to a child, "because they're members of the judicial council. Now are we done here?"

"Right, um, okay, yes. I'll—I'll let myself out."

"You do that. I suppose I'll be seeing you at the lodge later?"

"Funny, a little birdie told me that you weren't leaving the house much recently," Harry provokes.

"Little birdies do like to chirp, don't they?" his father fires back. "I forgot to ask, how was your Thailand trip, Harry?"

"*Goodbye*, George."

Jack quietly backs away from the door, throwing himself around the bannister at the top of the stairs and down several of them before the study door clicks open. He loiters a little, taking the steps slowly, until the man shoulders past him quickly with a shifty backwards glance.

Jack rubs his eyes blearily. "Uh, hey?"

"Jack, right?"

"Yeah, have we met?"

Harry gives him a strange look, tight and unhappy; Jack actually knows his face but can't place it. "Lotta years ago."

Harry takes the rest of the stairs, allowing one of the PMCs to frisk him, and Jack takes a quick trip to the kitchen, hearing the door slam on Harry's way out.

Jack grabs orange juice from the fridge and gulps it straight from the carton.

People are coming to the house now, he supposes, because his dad hasn't left the building since that night and he still has business to do. Business with judges, ostensibly.

Judges who're getting paid.

And again, it's not like Jack's at all surprised by this, but every little revelation, every uncovering of some truth that seems like it should be a given, still feels like its chipping something away from him. It's one thing to passively acknowledge that his father is a corrupt prick—it's another to come face to face with the more tangible realities of it. Federal bribery, for instance.

He heads back upstairs and into his room, and his laptop sits like a bright temptation on the desk, every instinct forged into him by nature itching to google the shit out of Harry-whoever.

The note so threateningly delivered by Jack's new assassin friend specified research, and for all anyone knows, Jack could just be cruising this guy on OkCupid.

It's a flimsy rationale. He agonizes over it a while, the desperate masochism that must be involved in subjecting himself to more of this. He deserves to know, he realizes; deserves both selfishly and as punishment to know the things he's left to grow under his mom's roof.

It's just a name, anyway. It's nothing of any real consequence.

His search brings up several Harrys appointed to courts in this district and the websites show him their pictures. His father's visitor is Harold McKouen, and a search of his name gets him more hits of the same, more corruption.

Judge Harold McKouen lost control of the gallery today after declaring a sentence of eighteen months' probation for businesswoman Beth Glossier for decades of fraudulent property conversion—

—surprise acquittal of LowTek CEO and alleged spousal murderer overseen by Judge Harold McKouen.

Is Harold McKouen a crook? Living the lavish life in his hillside manor, he's got people wondering: does a life of law really pay those bills?

The weight of his myopia crushes him. All these years fighting a battle of one with his father whilst outside these walls a war's been raging.

She'd said to him *Don't abandon him, baby,* and he'd told her *Sure, Mom, anything you want,* and she'd known how he'd considered it, known before Jack that what he was and what his father wanted were two entirely different animals. But things between them weren't the worst they could be just then, and without Jack's mom, without George's wife, all they had was each other.

And then his dad was gone all the time, inducted into a prestigious lodge, aspiring for newer and higher positions, and all Jack had was a promise.

He needs a damn drink or something, to get out of this house and away from the oppressive thumb of eyes and ears everywhere. He needs air and the kind of easy company his friends can offer, but there's no way a request to head to Sol's is going to go down well with his father, and the way Jack's feeling right now, oddly betrayed and stupid for his wilful ignorance, an actual fight with his dad just isn't safe.

So he waits.

He wastes time on canvases at the window of his bedroom, creating nothing but generic landscapes one after the other and the antithesis of what he really wants to put to paper, the stuff that decorates the South Plaza bars and protest pamphlets. He paints a forest, a sky at night, a waterfall, a beach, all in weird monochrome pallets, muted greens and grayish mauves. He could probably sell these for a quick buck, send them off to hang in lobbies or scan and print them for homeware stores.

He eats toasted sandwiches with Joel and Charlie on the outside bench while the sky sits patchy above them, mixed like paint on his board: gunmetal gray swirled with white and splotched against silvery blue, bright linings gilding everything.

And then, as promised, his father leaves for the lodge for the first time since the break-in.

A nondescript black car comes for him at eight-thirty and he's quickly hoarded into it with an armed detail. Jack watches them pull away from the lounge window, realizes after a while he's anxiously *waiting* for something bad to happen before he snaps himself out of it.

At nine-fifteen, Regina disappears into one of the guest bedrooms for a nap, and Jack dresses himself in dark jeans and boots and a black hoodie and makes like his seventeen-year-old self, scaling the back drainpipe from the second-floor bathroom.

It's only a moderately weak point in that it's simple enough to slide down, but the eight-foot drop toward the bottom all the way to the ground makes climbing up without something pretty large to stand on all but impossible; Jack's tried it dozens of times over the years and gotten nothing but injuries for his trouble.

He'll just have to take his punishment like his seventeen-year-old self, too, when he rocks up to the front door later.

He hops down as quietly as he can into the backyard bushes, and he's lucky—the wind is up, whipping out a static white noise. The back door guys smoke hand-rolled cigarettes a dozen yards away and laugh over something lost to the breeze, and Jack keeps low and vaults the back wall, escaping down the street and into the archway alley between two houses that brings him out onto the front road.

The surveillance van sits parked against the sidewalk some dozens of feet away and he slips out quickly, hands stuffed in his pockets and hood up, getting all the way out of sight across the road and around the corner of the wrought-iron park fence. Jack considers, for a second, calling a cab to Sol's, but the idea doesn't really gel with his bid for freedom, so he screws it.

Instead, he heads into the park just as the Windsor lamps start to light up the evening, turning the air sepia and the path warm and grainy.

Finally, *finally*, he can take a breath that doesn't smell like old wood or scented PlugIns.

Freedom tastes like ozone and bitter greens, today's fresh-cut grass spiraling up into little whirls with the wind. Jack melts into it, weather the warm side of mild even with the breeze, and the feeling of truly being alone in all this open space cutting the tense bowstring of his spine.

He approaches the thoroughfare in a daze, drugged off the powerful sensation of gravity tugging him home, and the shadowy figure he spots halfway down doesn't concern him for half a minute or so while he happily indulges himself.

Until suddenly it does.

His steps falter but don't stop, axis of gravity abruptly shifted, and now Jack's walking toward the figure instead, in the grip of some terrible, warped sense of inevitability with his heart rate kicking up.

His boots against the ground feel like a march, and he finds he's angry. Fraught with fear, yeah, but angry nonetheless. Worse, it's a petty anger, a kind of outrage that's got him thinking *how dare you* even though he's almost positive he brought this one on himself.

The figure stands with his stance wide and easy and his hands in the pockets of his leather jacket, casual as anything. He's wearing All Stars and Jack has to be fucking hallucinating right now, spent too long obsessing over this with no exposure to the outside world to ground him.

The figure tells Jack, "Hey," thoroughly doing away with *that* notion.

"*Hey?*"

The Goddamn *assassin* raises his eyebrows. "It's a term of greeting."

"Yeah, thanks," Jack snaps. "Gotta say, it's a massive improvement from your first one."

The guy shrugs a shoulder, mouth quirking up at one corner, and *fuck*, Jack had somehow forgotten how striking he was. Under the sodium lampposts, standing against the gray-shaded sugar maples, he's almost otherworldly—or maybe that's just Jack's abused brain whirring, fever-pitched imagination running wild with him like a kid let out for the first time on its own.

"Is this it, then?" Jack goes on, still dripping in sarcasm. "Time to say my prayers?"

"Walk with me?"

Jack does an honest-to-God spit-take, levelling a glare. "Walk with you."

"You can keep repeating what I say if you like."

Jack does, thanks. "*Walk with you?*"

"You haven't gone running to your armed guard for help," he points out and then, with a quiet weight, "It's important."

I'm sorry about this. Jack hears it over and over, a litany always inhabiting him, and this man had stood in his father's study with a *gun*, apologizing for a murder he was a split-second away from committing. Two days ago he'd handed Jack a threatening note, *flirting* with him while he did it.

Jack shakes his head. He wrenches himself away, one, two steps, turning his back on the face that's been dogging him for a week now because if he doesn't—

"Jack."

If he doesn't, Jack's going to do something like fucking walk with him.

Back still turned, Jack states the very obvious. "You know my name."

"Lotta people know your name. Your real one, anyway."

He spins at that. "How did you—"

"This is important," the man repeats gravely, but there's still an easiness to his stance, a kind of open appeal. He's drawing Jack in just like the flirting; good at his job, Jack thinks dizzily.

"Tell me your name, first."

He doesn't answer right away, sound of nothing but the trees swaying while he looks up at Jack with his head tipped down—*really* good at his job, then. There's a definite reluctance there, but beyond that, Jack really can't guess what he's thinking; maybe games of chess in his head, working out moves and countermoves, assessing Jack for danger.

"Alex."

Jack tries it out in his mouth—"Alex"—and finds it suits him whether it's real or not. "Fine, *Alex,* let's walk."

Alex cocks his head, gesturing to the end of the thoroughfare so Jack supposes they're heading away from the house and out into the city. A small mercy, at least.

They fall into step, Alex tossing Jack curious little sideways glances but otherwise staying perfectly quiet, until they come out onto the boulevard and under the open night sky, clear except for the spotty clouds moving time-lapse fast in the lower atmosphere.

There, Alex belatedly speaks. "You've been drawing attention to yourself."

"That an art pun?"

Another curious glance and Jack stays looking resolutely forward; he's really not sure indulging himself *or* this guy is the right thing to do.

"Maybe. Thanks for the sketch, by the way."

"Oddly polite for someone who handed me a threat in return."

"Which you didn't take seriously."

"So that is why you're here, because I googled some asshole judge?"

"Look, Jack—"

Jack immediately bristles. "Why am I drawing attention to myself? What's so important that you gotta follow me around town and spirit me away into the night like this, after you—after you tried to fucking—"

"I was sent to give you the note," Alex interrupts, carefully placing every syllable like they're practiced. "I wasn't sent tonight."

Jack turns his head, trying to get some sort of equal footing here. "And what does that mean?"

"I'm trying to help you."

"You—you're trying to—" Jack chokes a laugh, tripping over his words with how *not* funny this is. "I gotta tell you, this right here"—he gestures, encompasses everything—"doesn't feel like helping."

Alex slips out in front of him, turning to block Jack's path. "Look, I'm not even supposed to be here," he says roughly, some of his easy demeanor definitely snapping. "Consider this a courtesy call."

It's Alex's turn to walk away, and Jack's *almost* stubborn enough to let him, but his curiosity is lethal and his attraction whetted and cabin fever has made him restless, galvanizing him. He's so damn sick of feeling adrift.

"Hey," he calls out, steeling his resolve. "Say I believe that." Alex turns side-on, head angled against his shoulder. "You want my dad dead, right? So why help me?"

"You're not your father."

Jack scoffs, closing the gap Alex created. "So that gives me the right to live."

"I don't make that decision," Alex says flatly.

"Then who does?"

"You know I can't tell you that."

"Not even for the price of a walk?" Jack asks lightly, and Alex raises an eyebrow.

"Not even that."

"Well I'm heading downtown, and despite whatever you are, I don't think you just poof into thin air when I turn my back, right?"

"Right," Alex drawls. "That's the one thing lacking from my resume."

"Am I allowed to know where you're heading?"

Alex's smirking now. "Why, you wanna walk some more?"

"I could use a chaperone like you." Jack leans down conspiratorially. "Apparently my life's in danger."

The smirk becomes a chuckle, just a split-second thing, and it pleasantly stuns Jack, knocks all the air out of his lungs.

"You're pretty morbid, you know that," Alex idly comments, oblivious to the sucker punch he just delivered. "Most people don't joke about this kind of stuff."

Jack gestures a hand out over the boulevard, universal sign for *shall we*, but Alex keeps on scrutinizing him, amusement coloring a more unreadable expression, something sharply calculating and still hesitant. He wonders if this is a fraternizing-with-the-enemy thing, that Alex is scared of putting a personality to the life he or his associates are attempting to tear apart. The more Jack can forcibly confront him with it, the better.

"I don't bite," Jack adds.

"No," Alex agrees, slanting him an upward look. "You didn't."

Jack flushes hot, pressing his tongue against the backs of his teeth hard at the liquid rush of it. "Now look who's joking."

It appears to disarm Alex; he cocks his head, setting a walking pace again, Jack falling into step as he learns to navigate this stranger.

Seems they're forgoing transport, turning right onto the wide main street that cuts right through the heart of the whole north city, empty and gray this far uptown at night, but Jack can see the far-off intersection lights flashing.

Apparently, Alex doesn't want to take the well-traveled road, though, reaching out for an aborted second like he might tug on Jack's hoodie and turning the movement smoothly into a finger pointed down a side street.

"I guess we're staying off the radar," Jack jokes.

"You're not that far off."

"*Wow.*"

"It's dead out here, and we're still a little close to your place, it's just a precaution."

"You were serious," Jack marvels. "And you're—what? Disobeying orders or something?"

For me, he doesn't say, but it's a near thing.

"Something like that." Alex shrugs.

It's darker here, surrounded on both sides by Edwardian buildings, more townhouses and apartments for the middling wealthy. This whole block is a parochial rabbit warren of impenetrable brickwork, and if Alex was going to kill him or lead him into a trap, this would be a convenient spot.

Jack's pretty sure his great-aunt lives somewhere nearby.

"What happens if we get caught?" he asks.

"We won't."

"You're pretty confident about that for a guy who came here to warn me about my safety, who works for people who use military grade silencers on their—I'm pretty sure it was an MK-23."

Alex looks at him, eyebrows raised. "Impressive."

"You've got it on you right now, haven't you?"

"I'd be a pretty terrible chaperone if I didn't."

Alex's mouth is turned up at the corner, wry and teasing, and Jack's blood is up now, more than the thrill of reckless freedom from before. It's ancient and primal—fear, but the kind he wants to throw himself into to test those evolutionary boundaries.

It's Jack at his very worst, or his very best, depending on who you ask.

They pass under a streetlamp glowing down like a floodlight, and once he's in it, it's hard not to take a long, hard look at the man walking beside him.

Jack turns and puts out an arm, almost catching Alex in the crook of his elbow. He drags a hand to the middle of Alex's chest and walks him backwards into the lamppost, pressing and holding him there where he's lit up bare.

Alex doesn't fight; that fact isn't kind to Jack, thrilling sharply down his spine to settle dense and crackling in his stomach. Alex simply cocks his head back a little to look Jack in the eye, has to because of their difference in height; another fact that racks Jack senseless.

Alex asks, "What?" with that damned quirk to his mouth, still.

"What kinda crazy are you, exactly?" Jack asks. "Fringe or state-sanctioned?"

"Why do you keep asking question you know I can't answer?"

"Because I'm stubborn like that."

Jack's hand is still splayed in the middle of Alex's chest, zipped leather jacket getting in the way of any kind of actual intimacy so he decides to leave it there. He's pushing his luck plenty tonight; may as well wring every drop from it.

"Wouldn't be here if you weren't," Alex agrees amicably, and it rattles Jack, that he's so unflappable in the face of Jack getting in his space like this.

He remembers wide eyes in the pitch dark, the feel of an eager pulse against his thumbs. He messed this guy up, made the assassin on a mission forget himself, and no amount of calm can change what Jack knows.

"How about," Alex goes on, "you think up something I *can* answer."

"And will you?"

"It's kind of how a conversation works."

Jack raises his eyebrows, hearing a challenge. "Are you

single?"

Alex blinks, taking a quick breath that makes his chest expand all the way against Jack's palm, and Jack presses his mouth together, trying not to smirk. Surprise suits him, and Jack would hazard a guess that it doesn't happen all that often.

"Yes, I'm single."

Jack drums his fingers against the leather jacket, little tapping sounds in the silence, before he removes it entirely, stepping back a foot where the air feels clearer. "That could be a lie, though."

"Pretty pointless lie."

"Depends on what you're up to here."

Alex mouths a silent *ah* in realization. "That's not exactly in my job description."

"So it's just for me then?" Jack asks self-deprecatingly, and Alex looks away—away and then back up again, eyes briefly skipping against Jack's mouth.

"Is that an actual question, or—" He drifts off coolly and Jack senses a definite boundary; it bothers him, even though it shouldn't.

"No, it's not."

Jack starts to walk again, Alex falling back into step beside him.

"Okay, start easy: where'd you grow up?" he asks, pulling them back to safe ground, but then Alex kicks up a puddle and the movement is so young-seeming. "Wait, no, scratch that. How old are you?"

"I grew up on St. Ivan's Street," Alex tells him—a real poor area, even back when Jack was a kid. "And I'm twenty-nine."

"You're *my* age."

"You're perceptive."

"No, I—" Jack huffs. "I mean, you're my age and you, y'know, do this."

Alex shrugs, turning them onto a new street heading south. "Some twenty-nine-year-olds are nuclear physicists; some are Olympic athletes."

Jack doesn't point out the fundamental flaw with the logic of comparing a perfectly sane career with killing people. "Some are struggling artists?" he asks rhetorically instead.

"You wouldn't be struggling if you worked under your real name."

"If you saw half the stuff I make, you wouldn't be saying that."

"I have, actually," Alex says simply. "Your political satire? It'd mean a hell of a lot more coming from the son of the guy you're tearing apart."

Jack flushes a little, heat prickling the back of his neck. Only Sol and Shawn could put his name to that stuff. "I paint landscapes, too."

Alex chuckles. "You rebel."

"It's not like I don't wish I could come out of the proverbial art closet."

"Then why don't you?"

"Because my relationship with my dad is strained enough, thanks," Jack snaps.

Alex holds up both hands in a placating gesture. "Hey, it's none of my business."

"You sure seem to be making it your business."

"You brought it up," Alex points out.

They come to the end of the thinning residential area, passing by the school, the post office, the huge multi-story parking lot looming up ahead that means they're close to Laurel Street.

"Let's just call our jobs off-limits and leave it at that, huh?" Jack suggests, not even once considering parting ways might also be a viable suggestion, but—whatever; he's not too keen to end this just yet.

"Okay, sure."

They hit Laurel Street like a sudden supernova, stepping out from the sleepy hive onto the pumping vein of the mid-city. Speeding headlights cut through the dark, flashing intersections blinking as far as he can see in either direction. East, the psychedelia thickens, the blazing reds and yellows of cheap open restaurants and street-front shops that never close.

Without any joint consideration, they turn east and stroll in silence a while. It bugs him even though he kind of forced it, and before he can lose his nerve, Jack nudges Alex with his shoulder.

Alex turns his head, face impassive and then not, cracking into a droll smile that agitates the butterflies in Jack's stomach. He nudges Jack back, asking him, "So, where's this place I'm escorting you to?"

"A friend of mine runs a bar on the South Plaza," Jack starts, chewing his lip a second before he goes on, "but, uh, I just wanted to get outta the house, y'know? Escape. It wasn't about a specific destination."

"So you ditched your security."

"I was going stir-crazy, man."

"Still, not exactly smart or safe."

"Bumped into you, didn't I?"

Alex huffs, turning his face down; Jack thinks he might've hit a nerve. "Yeah, my point exactly."

"This a personal distinction or a professional one?"

"Thought we weren't talking about our jobs," Alex muses. "Your rule."

"I'm bending it."

"I see—you made the rule; you can break the rule."

"Little more like my father than you thought, huh?" Jack drawls, and Alex glances at him, quick and startled, and then he throws back his head and laughs, unabashedly delighted by that.

"I just do not get you," Alex tells him, still laughing.

"That's 'cause you've known me in person for like an hour, altogether."

"Nah, you bugged me on paper way before this."

Jack takes a second to process that. If he asks, he's likely to get shot down again, so instead he quips, "Obviously you like a good mystery, then."

They cross over at the intersection, hitting the crowds: the roving gangs of teenagers with nowhere better to hang out and the couples walking hand in hand, the men and women in business attire eating food on the go after a late shift at the office. Jack's a stray by nature, wandering and always fascinated with the individual details of these people, seeing moments of vibrancy in the mundane and wanting to capture it somehow like a pretty insect in a jar. His assumption for Alex is really just a reflection of himself, boils down this whole mad journey of theirs into a single issue.

"I'm partial," is Alex's answer, slanting Jack a look against the bright canvas of diners and burger vans.

Like before under the streetlamp, he can see it clearly: the exact shade of green of Alex's eyes. He knows how he'd mix it in paint, fingers itching for a brush suddenly. He wants to see Alex by sunlight, without his cap and shades, to map and color him precisely.

Vibrancy in the mundane; Jack's found the walking, talking definition.

"You want a soda or something?" Jack asks, bringing them to a halt on the sidewalk by the side of a truck. He thinks he might be trying to keep Alex in this light, just for a little while. "My treat."

"Um, sure?"

"You look like a Pepsi kinda guy."

Alex humors him. "Add some Jack and you'd be right on the money."

Jack eyes up the liquor store ten feet away. "I think I can manage that."

Two Pepsi cans and a pocket-sized bottle of Jack Daniel's purchased, Jack eagerly watches Alex crack open his soda and gulp some down before tending to his own. He shares the whiskey out, carefully trickling it into the drinks, and Alex holds his up in a toast.

"To drinking in the streets."

Jack taps the cans together. "With interesting company."

"*Interesting.*"

"Oh, definitely." Jack leans in closer, lowering his voice to quietly joke, "I'm calling my next piece: Assassin with a Can."

"So, I'm inspiring as well as interesting," Alex murmurs back, inching into Jack's space while the closeness and gently delivered quip gang up to daze him.

"Inspiring is one word."

Alex clicks his tongue. "Now, I don't know whether to take that as a compliment or not."

Jack laughs, stepping back and nudging them into a leisurely stroll. "Your call, man."

"I better get to keep it."

"Assassin with a Can? Sure, put it with the other thing. You can start a collection." Dryly, he adds, "Since you're such a fan."

Alex holds up his Pepsi, index finger raised. "Hey, I didn't say I was a fan."

"Actions speak louder than words."

He doesn't want to think about the fact Alex used his sketch as an in to hand him a threatening note. Seems Alex might be thinking the same thing, too, gone quiet with his head ducked. They can't avoid the huge, peripheral dose of reality that keeps encroaching on this sprawling nighttime fantasy, but Jack's sure as hell going to keep trying for a little while longer.

"You want inspiration, I have just the thing," Alex says, a little forced in its nonchalance, and he steers them down another side street.

It's a little dingy upward slope, blocked off from Laurel Street by the tall buildings. The whole road is dark cobblestone, uneven footing and some still slippery with the rain earlier, and Alex leans into him to point to a shadowed building up ahead.

As they get closer, Jack can see it looks burned out and graffitied, with layers and layers of paint betraying years of disuse, and wooden boards nailed over the front doors and low windows. Its front and side are latticed in scaffolding but the architecture underneath is lovely, Renaissance-style white stone with domed towers.

Jack's never taken any notice of it before, and he feels,

suddenly, like a guest in his own city. It's a wholly unfamiliar sensation, gripping him pleasingly and appealing to his fascination. It's one thing after another with Alex, it seems.

"They called it the Gaumont. It was a theatre," Alex explains, reaching high to put his drink on a wooden scaffold platform. "There was a fire here eighteen years ago." He grips a metal pole and pulls himself up with a lovely amount of easy grace, dipping into a crouch and holding a hand out to Jack. "Coming up?"

"Is this even safe?"

"When you see the view, you won't even care."

Jack shakes his head, helplessly grinning. He passes Alex his drink instead of his hand, getting his footing against the crisscrossing metal and climbing up, reconsidering his impossible stance on that drainpipe back home; if anyone could climb the thing, Alex probably could.

He gestures along the platform, telling Jack, "The view from the other side is better," and Jack takes it slowly, cringing at the creak of warped, old wood as they clamber up two more levels.

He clings to the rail, carefully rounds a corner, and climbs the upward slope until they reach a stone balcony where the scaffolding takes a break. Alex hops down, still holding both cans, and Jack slips down after him, glad to have something more solid underneath his boots.

The balcony is pretty big, a large sweeping curve where the stone barrier looks over the street below and then further: a view of the city that Jack didn't expect, the grimy little streets like a maze, and then the twinkling lens-flare of Laurel Street in all its vivacious glory stretching as far as the fuzzy shape of the distant river.

"I've never even heard of this place," he says quietly, touching the smooth, rounded top of the stone railing.

"It was built in the thirties as a music venue and ballroom, and then later it doubled as a movie theatre," Alex tells him softly. "The city keeps trying to tear it down, but the people keep fighting for it."

"Inspiring." Jack repeats the sentiment, giving Alex a sideways glance. "You weren't wrong."

Alex hands him his drink and toasts him, taking a long gulp and leaning a hip against the rail. "You'll find no better place in the city to drink JD and Pepsi from a can like a teenager."

Jack laughs. "Speaking from experience?"

"Oh, yeah, I used to do this all the time. Sometimes me and my buddies would break in—well"—he flaps a hand at the glassless balcony doors with torn blue sheets draped over them—"*walk* in."

"How come it's still like this?"

"Nobody official can decide what to do with it, so they just let it sit out here and rot."

Jack thinks that what Alex isn't saying outright is that George Preston's hand is firmly in this willful neglect, and Jack wonders if that's another courtesy he's been afforded. He's struck again with the strangeness of the night, like his better senses are way back uptown where the city is falling asleep, instead of here where it's just waking up.

"See that 7-Eleven way, way down there?" Jack points into the distance. "Used to be craft store, bought all my art supplies from there for years."

Alex raises an eyebrow. "You trying to one-up my nostalgia points?"

The alcohol is working its magic now, smudging hard-to-quantify concepts into softer amusements and easy forgetfulness. "I once shoplifted an eraser from there when I was ten and freaked out about it so much I went and put it back the next day."

"That definitely wasn't in your record," Alex laughs.

"My record," Jack scoffs. "All the campaign attention all these years does not even compare to how weird it is that you've read a record about me."

"If it helps, it's not very invasive at all. You're not exactly the, uh, subject in question."

"I'm not my father?" he echoes.

"Well, you're not."

"And what about you? What're your parents like?"

Alex leans his elbows against the stone, gazing out over the cityscape. "The apple fell pretty far from that tree, too."

"So your dad doesn't break into people's houses with guns, then?"

"I mean he might have, but not that I know of," Alex jokes, and then, "He used to work at the docks, loading up the boats. Mom was a seamstress."

"Was?" Jack asks gently.

"My mom was, but she doesn't need to do that now."

Because Alex's job keeps her well provided for, is what he doesn't say, but Jack hears it anyway. What he does is a well-paying career, then, and that could mean a lot of things: more private military, government, political opposition. Narrows the scope a little, though, and while Jack didn't exactly *think* Alex was dedicated to some kind of extremist cause, he can't imagine those things are particularly well paying.

It feels like a puzzle now, a game, and that is dangerous in itself. That Alex didn't clarify about his father is another piece.

"Any brothers or sisters?"

"Sister, college out of state. You trying to build a profile on me?"

Jack laughs. "If I was, I'm sure your buddies monitoring my internet will let you know."

The warm wind whips up again, flapping the plastic sheets and rattling the scaffolding, carding blissfully through Jack's hair. He leans back against the rail, tipping his head back into the airflow, eyes closed and feeling dizzy with that one sense blinked out while all the rest scale up to eleven.

When Alex speaks, the directness of his voice tells Jack he's looking right at him. "So, Hollis Porter."

Jack groans. "Thought I was the only one who could break the job discussion rule."

"I'm invoking my right as a citizen to contest it, on the grounds of elitism or something."

He doesn't open his eyes, the sense that Alex is so close and looking up at him heady and vivid. "Elitism, *or something*."

"Shut up."

"The day I moved out the townhouse, it was like the fucking O.K. Corral, hours of yelling, throwing stuff, I thought we were gonna kill each other for sure." Jack smirks, blindly, into the sky. He hears Alex huff. "He was convinced me living in some crappy downtown apartment, making my own way, painting for a living, was gonna ruin him somehow."

"I figured the pseudonym was good for the satire; I didn't get the need for the more generic stuff."

"He would've shut me down before I'd gotten a foot out the door. It's a compromise that we never talk about, I guess. Don't get me wrong, I get by," he admits. "The waterfall landscape hanging in the Lorabelle Hotel bought groceries for five weeks. The political stuff is a great side project but I didn't plan on it—it just happened because someone asked."

"And then you kept doing it?"

"This old girl who owns a bookshop in the plaza, real anarchist type, she was the first. Some of her buddies caught on, and suddenly, I was painting my dad as an eighteenth-century French nobleman on the front of a two-dollar bill. And she didn't even know who I was."

He can hear Alex's smile when he says, "I liked that one," and then Jack *can't* keep not looking at him.

He opens his eyes to the clouds, takes a breath of it, and then turns his head against his shoulder, into the new view of Alex's curious, upturned eyes.

There is something so terribly wanton about this man, he thinks. He's a poised figure, professionally confident, with a face that slips too easily into a smirk and a manner subtly unwholesome. Presentable to a point and then exposed depths of potential disrepute.

"I knew you were a fan," Jack jokes, so quiet in that nothing space between them, Alex's shoulder brushing Jack's and his face right fucking *there*.

"I think you downplay yourself," Alex quips back. "Maybe you need a few more fans like me."

He finds himself roughly muttering, "If I had fans like you," and Jack hits the brakes on that thought *so damn fast*, clearing his throat, looking away from the minute reactive interest on Alex's face. "Being relatively unknown is safer anyway."

"For your father's reputation, not for living in this expensive-ass city."

"It's a balance I gotta work with."

"I've wondered a while," Alex starts, hesitating in Jack's peripheral vision. "Your dad's got money to burn, why doesn't he—"

"Give me lots of cash?"

"Yeah."

"He used to try, but I didn't want him to own me."

"I don't mean this disrespectfully," Alex starts, homespun, *aw-shucks* kind of grin trying to blind Jack to what will most likely be something that sounds disrespectful.

"That's right up there with *no offence, but,*" Jack points out.

"True, but I'm honestly not."

"Go on, then."

"You still talk to him." Alex feels animated, eager beside him. "You still head back home when he needs you for PR."

"I promised—" *My mom;* fuck, Jack almost said it, just like that, like it was the easiest thing to share and not a fact that Sol and Shawn had to work for. He swallows down the words, clearing his throat. "He's still my dad," Jack settles on.

He sees Alex nod slowly, thoughtful and emotive, and Jack thinks he's gonna say something, but he waits and waits, and it doesn't come. Just time pending, heightening moments while Alex watches him, and Jack waits for the punch line like he's waiting for a punch.

Eventually Jack breaks, making struggling eye contact. "*What?*"

"Nothing, just piecing together my mystery is all."

Jack's charmed by the word choice, against his better intentions. "Care to share?"

Alex shrugs his shoulder, leather catching the material of Jack's hoodie. He sips down what sounds like the last dregs of his drink. "Maybe later."

"I'm holding you to that."

"You can. The night is young, and I still gotta get you to your bar."

Jack feels a layering of grief over descending the scaffolding, the finality of moving away from such a unique experience too close to waking up. Up there they were static in time and secluded away, down here they have to keep on going until the end of the line.

But the air is lazier on the ground, muggy and close, and Alex unzips his jacket with a smirk that says he knows Jack's paying attention; it's a new kind of joint wonder, tempting in its mutual unfolding.

They head back out under the bright lights and onward into the night.

Chapter Six

They stroll the kinetic pinks and blues of Laurel Street, past the takeouts opening up for the nighttime bar scene and checkered with dark empty stores made derelict by hiking rent prices.

Laurel Street is middle ground, an indeterminate fusion of new and old that regularly shifts in its bones and can't seem to find a form that sits. Lately, Jack can sense the risk-aversion happening; too many people burned when big dreams of creating something different fall apart and leave them broke.

Once the settle finally happens, he imagines either perfect uniformity or total decay. Places south of the river thrive off cheap thrills and decades of well-established goodwill, but up here, the goodwill is conditional and the money always in flux.

The rain starts to mist down in sheets, finely soaking and driving people into shelter, and Alex pulls him into a tiny corner place with soccer scarves on the wall and smokers huddled under the back door awning, smell of it creeping inside and mixing with the damp floorboards.

There's a few rumbles of thunder, the promise of that storm that hasn't delivered yet, and they drink beer and argue sports until the sky clears again, blown out by the wind picking up.

Jack learns—to absolutely zero surprise—that Alex used to play soccer and baseball and athleticism basically lives and breathes in him. Jack admits his disdain for all things organized, like Alex hasn't already figured that out yet. Without the benefit of normal date protocol, or whatever the hell this fucking is, Jack's found his intuition is in overdrive, and he throws his theories out like darts at a board; yes, Alex is a dog person, and yes, he owns a motorbike, and no, he doesn't dance, except he clearly can with the sweet little flush on his cheeks.

Jack's grinning, draining his bottle. "You gotta admit, I'm pretty good at this."

"Are you after a job or something?" Alex asks him dryly, and they head outside onto the sidewalks all mirrored by rain, the huge M of the McDonalds across the road reflected like a red infinity sign.

"And if I was," Jack drawls, "who would I be applying to again?"

Laurel Street turns onto a road running parallel with the river and Jack doesn't expect an answer, but with all those intuitive senses super-changed, he absolutely expects the eye-roll he gets.

There's no way he should be able to read this man as well as he already can, and the fact that it could be a con, a clever ploy to gain Jack's trust, is distantly trying to make itself heard and far too easy to compartmentalize.

They descend the stone stairs to the footbridge running lower but parallel to the transport bridge, all the way down because the path is almost river-level, often flooded out of use by the rising water levels. It's badly lit but less battered by the gust funneled down the river, and Alex looks out over the rail and points. "Hey, look."

It's a small flock of colored Chinese lanterns caught in the wind, spiraling up and up and reflecting off the broken river surface.

An imminent goodbye is lodged underneath Jack's skin. He stands a foot behind Alex, watching the lanterns rise and caught in his own kind of airflow, the longing to step forward to see how Alex fits against him when they're not fighting.

He doesn't do it, obviously, but he could. He could, and he wonders what might happen then.

"Who d'you think let them go?" Alex asks, standing against the railing, and Jack shrugs before he remembers Alex can't see him.

He takes that step, hovering for a nothing second before putting them side by side.

Alex's shoulders tense and release accordingly.

"Probably a celebration or something," Jack says idly.

"Or a funeral."

"That's—morbid."

Alex smiles indulgently. "Now you're getting me."

His face looks sharp in this lighting, acutely intelligent and like he could scour the thoughts right out of Jack's head. It's gotta be a trick, how he fits brand new into every different piece of scenery; he's like a flip book—look away for a few seconds and you've missed some vital piece.

He's too Goddamned specifically tailored to Jack's exact weaknesses.

"What else is in that file about me?" Jack asks him, same idle tone.

"You like long walks on the beach and thunderstorms."

Jack rolls his eyes. "Cute." It's not a bad guess, though.

"Getting me a little better."

"I'm serious."

"Things that tie back to your father," Alex offers impatiently. "It's—it's fucked up, I know."

That, Jack wasn't expecting. "You know what I know now?" Alex shakes his head. "My dad pays off judges. Did you know that too?"

"I—"

"And I think he hires criminals."

Alex raises a silent eyebrow.

"You do know," Jack says flatly. "What I don't understand is why that ties back to me in any way, unless you think I'm in on it."

"Maybe you're just—interesting."

Alex takes the kind of breath that preempts more speech, but he blows it out with an awkward wince, almost apologetic.

Jack looks away. He wants to believe it's genuine, just like before, but he can't if he looks; Alex too disarming to disbelieve at a glance.

Jack quips, "Make a wish," up at the stray lanterns streaming over the bridge instead.

Alex steps to the side, behind Jack, making him spin around. He very briefly puts a hand between Jack's shoulder blades and points up at the lights illuminating the river bank. "Second star on the right and straight on till morning."

And then he's walking again, Jack lurching forward to catch up. "That's Peter Pan, idiot."

"And those are flying pieces of paper on fire."

Jack laughs, shaking his head, and they come out on the other side of the river where the plaza shines in the middle distance, vibrant with life.

"The Moonlight Mile never sleeps," he says fondly, after a long lull in conversation that's brought them almost to it; end of the line, Jack thinks, and he doesn't know how to talk about it or articulate what he actually wants, so he doesn't.

The plaza cobbles are slick under them, and he slows his walk, Alex matching the pace like they've been doing all night. Sol's bar isn't far now, and Jack feels another layer of grief added to the sodden blanket sensation pushing in over him.

"It's been a long time since I came down here," Alex tells him— weary, equally as fond, sounds like finality and smothers Jack heavier. "Too long."

"Yeah?"

"It's hard to find the time."

"Job keeps you busy, huh?"

Alex scoffs, answering shortly, "Very."

"Not busy enough that you can't take a few hours out to be a chaperone, though." Jack tosses him a glance. "Or am I keeping you from something?"

There's no reaction save Alex's tongue wetting his bottom lip.

"Don't tell me," Jack starts. "This is all a distraction, and there's someone blowing up my father's house right now."

Alex raises an eyebrow. "Implying that I'm currently saving your life for some unknown reason?"

Jack doesn't point out that Alex's self-admitted purpose tonight was warning him away from danger; although, yeah, now that he thinks about it, Alex still hasn't given Jack a reason.

"Unknown and nefarious."

"Say that's what's happening," Alex says lightly. "What nefarious reason does a guy have to save another guy's life?"

"That's the million-dollar question." When Alex doesn't offer anything else, Jack swallows thickly and goes on feeling far less charitable. "I'd be in your debt," he says quietly. "Way you were talking before, I might already be."

They pass the wicked indigo signage of the Blue Bell strip club, and Alex's mouth opens and closes a couple times, making botched words that don't come out.

Jack cringes, fisting both hands into his hoodie pockets. "What are we doing?"

"I don't know."

That sounded very much like a bubble breaking.

Alex reaches out an arm, halting Jack with the barrier of it. They face each other, eerie blue tinge over everything. The sinuous shape of a dancing girl behind a pane of glass in Jack's peripheral vision doesn't add any kind of sensibility to the proceedings; Jack's well and truly down the rabbit hole.

"Look. You're not at all," Alex says and then clarifies, "In my debt, I mean. In anyone's debt. And nobody's blowing the house up, but—*fuck*—" He scrubs a hand over his mouth, pinching his bottom lip between two fingers. "There's a lot of shit I know, and a lot of shit I don't, but yes, there are files on you, and yes, people want your father dead, and none of that has or is going to change."

It's raw in its candidness, the most blunt Alex has been on the subject, and Jack wishes he was articulate enough to reconcile the familiar cobbles and sindustry lights with talking about a hit-job.

Feels disconcertingly like a movie, Alex the part of the shady criminal character with a dark past or whatever. What does that make Jack, he wonders. The stubborn dame who's in too deep?

His frustration is difficult to narrow down, to direct. "And your warning before means what, exactly?"

Alex looks him flat in the eye. "Don't end up on the shit list along with him."

"Okay," Jack says slowly, irreverent with sarcasm. "Close my eyes, stick my fingers in my ears, and the next time I see a guy in the shadows with a gun, just walk outta the room and leave him to it?"

Alex sighs and Jack thinks maybe, finally, he's pushed this whole thing to its logical limits; because it had to end, didn't it? There had to be a breaking point. They couldn't just exchange phone numbers and go to dinner and act like they were normal.

"For the love of God, don't tackle them again, at least," is what Alex wearily replies.

It's a cyclical debate that Jack just isn't going to win. There's no insight to be gained here when the stakes are a fucking secret, and the danger of it eludes him in ways Alex is obviously acutely aware of.

"*Them.*" Jack huffs a caustic laugh. "Right, they won't send you again because you fucked up."

Alex's expression hardens. "That's correct."

Now Jack's being *addressed,* and with a clipped formality. It hits a nerve, makes him feel petulant and he hates that. Hates being in the dark, too; hates unfocused confrontation with no possible resolution. What he hates most of all is that his lack of tangible direction forces the whole mess of complicated issues specifically onto Alex; knowing the guy just a few days has tipped Jack's entire world on its axis.

"And when they do send someone who can get the job done, my dad's gonna be dead."

He's set to feel viciously satisfied with that blow, but Alex responds so abruptly, so suddenly furious, that the satisfaction dies somewhere around Jack's ribcage.

"*Someone* has to stop him."

They stare at each other. Jack replays the sentence in his head until it makes sense, and then it resonates like a punch to the jaw, seizing his spine with dread like a plucked string.

His throat cramps around his hoarse voice. "What has he done?" He sounds five years old—lost and insubstantial.

Alex looks fucking horrified and doesn't answer him, keeps on not answering until Jack realizes he's backing away, and Jack's all desperation and no common sense—grabbing for him, fists closing over Alex's open jacket, and the metal teeth of the zippers digging itchy against his palms.

"Don't."

Alex placates Jack with his own name, "Jack," just like that; the name in his mouth highly engaging for such a small thing. He takes a gentle hold of Jack's forearms, not pushing, not anything but touching. Touching Jack, lingering and purposeful for the first time all night, and he feels every warm curl of every finger through his hoodie. "That was—I shouldn't've said that."

"Fucking bribery," Jack says, panicked and too loud. He might be backing Alex up against the wall of a nearby bar, an eighties' retro-future poster for some electro band gaudy over his shoulders, but that could just as easily be Alex guiding them out of the main path of the street. "People don't get assassinated for being greedy, corrupt assholes. If they did, we'd be burying them by the millions."

"Jack," Alex tries again, softly pleading, and a stark counterpoint to Alex's grip on him turned vice-like. "Lower your voice."

Jack takes a rough breath, says through his gritted teeth, "I'm not being unreasonable."

"I know," Alex says earnestly, and completely expressive with it. "And I'm not being deliberately difficult."

Says it all, really—nicely summed up in a couple of shared breaths. A fortified stalemate he could butt his head against for the rest of his life and never break. He sighs, shuddery and defeated, unclenching his fists from Alex's jacket and just sort of hanging there, still holding on.

He can't pin down whether he prefers this right here, the bluntly exposed nerves of them, or the soft surrealism from before, the idle strolling and drinking and pretending.

"Just tell me something," Jack mutters, adding, "if you can," because it looks like Alex is about to argue again. "Why?"

"Why—"

Jack cuts him off with a glare. "Deliberately difficult, huh? Come on, why'd you wait out in the park for me tonight? What's it worth to you?"

They're in the shadow of the Moonlight Mile, tucked under the structure of some neon lettering and Alex's back to the grimy bricks and torn paper, and Jack can taste the tension, the ripples of it that thrum in the scant bit of space he's given Alex to walk away.

He could lean in.

He could lean in and screw the damn question, kiss Alex, get a hotel room, fuck this insanity out of both their systems and then forget this whole feverish night. Chalk it up to trauma making him wild, bringing out the worst in him.

But what Alex has to say might be the most important words uttered in all the English language for the way Jack's hanging on them like his dying breath.

"It's—worth a life," Alex tells him, more like he's asking a question than making a statement, but he meets Jack's gaze head on all the same.

"That's how it works, you take one, you save one?"

"No," Alex says—one hard, sure syllable. "I take plenty, no one ever gets saved."

"How—" Jack fumbles over the *no one* part, the living exception to the rule and all, but the question tears its way out despite that. "How many people have you killed?"

Alex's whole body hitches on something like a laugh but lacking any kind of amusement. His eyes snap away, out somewhere over the plaza, and he shakes his head, lips turning down at the corners in a sneer.

There's a whole lot of spit suddenly flooding Jack's mouth and he swallows thickly. "Jesus, this is, this is freaking *crazy*, what the hell am I—"

Finally, he releases Alex's jacket completely, backing away a few steps with his senses all just fucking hitting him at once along with Alex's honed and wary gaze, accepting his fate like Jack has any damn authority to deliver it.

This man is dangerous, he tells himself—not for the first time and probably not the last as he tries to navigate this separation.

Because Alex is so far off the beaten track of normal that Jack's ability to define him, to relate to him, is skewed beyond comprehension. He can see it in fits and starts, when the fantasy fades out and reality kicks in. The thread of attraction, or connection, is a rope just obscured enough to hang himself with.

"You don't have to trust me," Alex tells him flatly. "But you do need to believe me. Quit prying; just leave it alone. You don't wanna be a part of any of this."

Jack nods silently. He doesn't dare open his mouth to let things fall out because this is a goodbye if he's ever heard one, and logic dictates he walk away from this whole mess.

If he could just turn the hell around—*God,* but he can't, not in time, not before Alex is taking several steps forward to look up at him, light from the Mile dusting down to hit him like a damn holy offering.

"It's hardly worth a damn, but—I'm sorry."

Jack can vividly see himself telling Alex he has nothing to be sorry for, and he doesn't speak until he's positive that he's not that far gone.

"Yeah, I know."

Silence that's swollen like a bad ache piles up between them, and Alex belatedly breaks it, face smoothing out into a wry half smile. "See ya, Cinderella."

Impulsively, Jack checks his watch, a laugh choking out of him; it's just past midnight. "Yeah, see you."

Alex takes one last look, a raking up and down that makes Jack hot and sore all over, and then he turns and walks off into the night, down the electric plaza until he's lost in the crowds. Heading wherever he's heading, Jack realizing he'll never know.

"Well, then," he says to himself. "Okay."

He looks up at the sky, basically little more than a habit now, watching the low broken clouds stream sluggishly over his head; things moving on like they do, people passing him like he's little more than the background noise to their own stories.

He recognizes the emotion: emptiness. Hits him hard and right in the chest.

For a few hours he'd felt wired and impulsive, the buried little itch in him scratched. Alex may well be dangerous, but Jack's a perilous unknown, too much potential to ignite given the right fuel. Once his finger hits the self-destruct button, it's riveted there, and this pressure cooker he's living in right now is no place to indulge all his petty embers of rebellion.

Sol's isn't far, and it's that or heading back, retracing the steps he just took with Alex to get down here and suffering all of the fresh memories while they're still raw.

Jack can put on a blank expression and face his friends for a while. He'll face the real music back home later.

Chapter Seven

"So who is he?"

Jack rakes a hand through his hair. It's a mess, tangling between his fingers; he needs a shower and a change of clothes. He needs to go back to the townhouse.

"What makes you think there's even a he?" he mutters into his coffee, slouched back on Sol's sofa where he spent the night tossing and turning.

"You come into my bar and mope for two hours, get hammered and then crash out on my sofa." Sol's endless capacity for multi-tasking has her pacing the living room rubbing down a wet plate with a towel. "I know the drill, Jack."

She disappears into the kitchen, and he hears the plate join the rest with a clatter. She appears with another one, sudsy water dripping onto the floorboards.

"He's hot and unavailable, what more do you want from me?"

"He's hot and unavailable," Sol deadpans at her girlfriend.

"He's gotta be another politician's son, right?" Josie guesses, talking mostly to Sol from her tired curl in the armchair. "Or an actual politician."

"For fuck's sake, Jack." Sol heads back into the kitchen to ditch the plate. "Didn't you learn your lesson hard enough last time?"

"I didn't even say yes!"

It's a damn good cover, though, and the truth is infinitely more disturbing, so Jack lets them believe it.

Sol perches on the arm of Josie's chair. "Is he at least not married?"

"He's not married."

"Well that's something."

"Risky," Josie points out. "Right in the middle of your father's campaign."

"Oh," Sal breathes. "This is rebellion."

Jack pulls a face. "*What*? No."

Jesus, it's not, is it? Jack's not that un-self-aware, surely. Alex is—something. Fucking something, all right. Yeah, rebellion is a pretty powerful compulsion, but he's attracted to Alex in a way he hasn't been attracted to anyone in a long time.

Was. Was attracted to him.

"I never even got my hands on him," he admits.

He hasn't told Sol about his father's attack at all, about the PMC presence, about his whole sordid family business. Strict orders from the house, and even if he doesn't abide all of them, this one Jack's sticking too; there's no way he's bringing his friends into this clusterfuck.

"You haven't even kissed him?" Sol asks, exchanging a look with Josie. "Honey, are you sure he's even into you?"

Jack sighs. "It doesn't matter because like I said: unavailable. It's not happening, not ever."

"I wouldn't say never. You do fall pretty hard when the guy's all wrong for you."

That makes him huff a laugh. "Whatever, it's highly likely that I'll never see him again anyway."

Now he doesn't know if that's true, life being like it is right now, but it feels—important. To say that. To try to believe in it.

Josie clicks her tongue. "Do you know how bad I wanna know who this guy is now? Quit stirring my interest." She drains the last of her own coffee, balancing with a hand on Sol's leg to haul herself up to standing. "I gotta get to work, but if he spills anything—" She gestures a thumb at Jack. "Sol, you text me, okay?"

"Sure thing, sweetie," she drawls, kisses Josie a goodbye, and then they're left alone, Jack staring into the dregs in his mug, head aching something fierce. "I don't know, Jack. What are we gonna do with you, huh?"

"Put me out of my misery," he groans.

"I can't win with you, I've tried." Sol shimmies herself down into the empty armchair. "I tell you you're probably better off staying clear of this guy, you're gonna do nothing but obsess about him. If I encourage you to take a chance, you'll get bored of him within a month and I'll still be picking up the pieces."

"It's not like that this time." How can he—he can't. "God, you have no idea, Sol. Everything is such a mess right now, and I can't even explain it to you."

She frowns; he sounds awful even to his own ears. "Wait, you're really serious. Why not?" When he doesn't answer, she sharply prompts, "*Jack*, why not?"

"Because it's wrong." His voice is hoarse, and he swallows. "It's so wrong—him, what I'm doing, all of it."

He's upset her, he can tell, and he feels the cracks splitting in his own self, eyes stinging but too dry to well up.

"Jack, seriously, you're scaring me."

Last night is an indistinct blur after Alex, and Jack's fucked himself with this unnecessary hangover, entirely at the mercy of his undefended emotions. Within half a minute he's ashamed of himself for his vulnerability, and in half a minute more who fucking knows what.

"It's nothing."

"Bullshit."

"I mean it, Sol," he says, harder. "I'm being ridiculous, I'm fine."

"You were a mess after Richard Leigh," she reminds him, like that one mistake is the yardstick against which every subsequent fuckup has to be measured. "I thought you were gonna hurt yourself."

"I'm always a mess."

Sol clasps her hands between her knees and shakes her head. "No, you're not, you just use that as an excuse."

"'Mona, don't," he begs, cracking on the plea. She blinks at him, eyes wide. "Look, I should get back to my dad."

"Oh, hell no—"

"It's *fine*. It's gonna be worse if I don't."

"Let me give you a ride at least." It's not an offer—there's no room for brokering in this deal.

So he straps himself into her old Honda, flicking at the pine freshener and the little voodoo string doll hanging from the rearview. Sol hands him her coffee thermos and gets them moving, and he drinks from it, ignoring her pissy look.

It's halfway across town before she speaks again.

"Y'know," she says slowly, loaded. Jack tenses preemptively. "Hugh came in the bar the other day."

"Oh, *God*, not this—"

"Him and Eric broke up. He was asking about you."

"Hugh is the single dullest guy in Broneburg," he snaps. "And he's so far up his own ass, he can kiss his own uvula."

He can *hear* the eye-roll. "He's dull by your standards; by anyone else's, he's actually pretty normal." She reaches across, stealing back her thermos. "It's not a bad thing to come down to Earth sometimes, Jack."

"I don't do well on the ground," he says dryly. "Would you let me get over my last impossible love before you try to shove another one on me?"

"Who said anything about love? I heard he was killer in bed."

Jack scoffs, word choice aside, and he's so fond of her in that moment that he has to fist his hands in his lap to stop from reaching over. It's Sol who brings him down to Earth; nobody else is worthy of that job.

"Who'd you hear that from?"

"My sources are my own," she says enigmatically. "You could always confirm or deny, for the sake of research."

He considers it, but the thought's instantly like ash, fraily breaking up before it even takes a hold. He calls up an old and dependable image of Richard and finds it's the same kind of instant dismissal, completely unthinkable.

"Think I'll pass for now," he tells her. "Drop me off at the park, would you?"

"Your old man hates me way more than I deserve."

"You keyed the word *pride* into his BMW."

She turns the wheel, gesturing vaguely. "Yeah, ten years ago. He really needs to learn how to let go." They pull up beside the park and Jack leans over, pulling her into a quick one-armed hug. "You smell like my bar, get off me."

He leans back. "You know how much I love you, right?"

"Are you dying?" she asks incredulously. "I feel like you're trying to tell me you're dying."

"No, I'm—" He pulls a face, palming his forehead. "I'm not

fucking dying, oh my God, forget it."

"Go take a shower, sober up, and call me later."

"Got it."

He salutes her as a goodbye, hit by the crisp morning so hard he almost doubles over with the shock of it. Sol drives away, and his skin *aches* through the shiver of cold, too much, too fucking much.

Regina is not pleased to see him on the doorstep.

Charlie's too pleased, hiding a snigger as Jack gets chewed out.

"Are you trying to make my job difficult?" she asks him in the hall, slamming the front door on the show.

He looks at the floorboards. "No, ma'am."

"Then maybe you could explain your little Houdini act to your father so I don't get my ass handed to me."

"Wait, he actually noticed I was gone?"

"This morning, yeah."

The momentary surprise gives over to weariness. "This is so ridiculous."

She gives him a look like she knows this but keeps carefully silent on the subject, drawling instead, "You've got some time to come up with a story that makes me sound good at least. Your father's in some kinda meeting in the dining room with a bunch of people."

He smirks. "I went out the window."

Regina shakes her head, biting her lip around a grin. "You

little shit."

He tells her not to worry about it, he'll fix it, and then he heads for the shower to slough off the whole guilty affair, the dust of the city and the means to forget. He changes into something clean and falls back onto his mattress, shutting his eyes against the spinning ceiling and finding the psychedelic patterns on the insides of his eyelids doing much the same.

His dad will come for him when he's ready, Jack thinks grimly, and then, as he drifts a little, awkwardly too comfortable on the bed after a night on a sofa: *can't outrun the devil*. George, Alex, a gun, the truth.

Chapter Eight

"Irresponsible, selfish—"

It's nothing Jack hasn't heard coming out of his dad's mouth before, and at least, this time he feels deserving of the anger, but the whole tone of it, his dad speaking to him like he's eight years old, has always gotten his back up in the worst way. Jack rolls his eyes like he is *actually* eight years old, knowing how bad it'll get his dad's back up in turn.

"Do you not understand the gravity of this situation?" George seethes, cold light of morning making him look as stressed as he obviously is. "Is it so difficult for you to comprehend that some psycho tried to kill me?"

Jack fires back, "Seems like *some psycho* should be dealt with by the police, no?"

"Quit trying to weasel out of this," his dad says darkly.

"I am well aware that someone tried to kill you. I was there, remember? Saving your life!"

"That doesn't let you off the hook for acting like a child."

"I *said* I was sorry for not telling you, but this place is like a damn cage—"

"Well, you better learn to live in it. Suzanne from the Broneburg Review is setting up an interview soon, and I want you smart and on your best behavior."

"Great," Jack scoffs. "We're hiding an attempt on your life from the authorities, the house is full of PMCs, and you're inviting the press in for a chat."

"I still have a damn election to win. That doesn't change because of a few slipups."

Slipups.

Jack's glad of the ringing cellphone on his dad's desk, then. George snatches it up, jerking it to his ear and snapping, "What?"

His whole expression changes, drops, and Jack's stomach drops with it, because his physiology is so attuned to every landscape now, high-strung emotions dragging him to and fro.

His dad presses the phone to his chest and tells Jack, "This isn't over, get out," and Jack gladly does, slamming the door closed, the voice behind him telling the caller, "Tell him to get over here as soon as he can and make sure he's not seen," and "No, I can't fucking come to him," before Jack stalks away.

Boyce stands impassive in the corner of the hall, and Jack avoids his eyes as he walks, hates feeling judged by these people in his family home and only a little because he's judging himself, too.

He's at a loss again, doesn't know what the hell to do with himself. Life's all stop-start, last night's exhilaration riding so high, and now today's nothing leaving him hollow and mournful. The quiet moments after each storm are doing a number on his nerves.

He avoids the downstairs completely, no will for the milling people, shutting himself inside his time warp room to stare at the high school diploma still framed over the blue wallpaper, the photo collage he hung ten years ago and the silver-gray sheets still the same ones he fucked Frankie Nimtz on when he was seventeen years old.

Outside the rain lashes the stone walls and glass panes and inside his stomach tosses with restless energy. He paces a little, halting by the window every so often to get pissed off at how dark it is for midday, while he tries to steer resolutely clear of his laptop.

Jack asks himself: if his choices were free, what would he want right now?

For his dad to be safe. For his dad to respect him. Or for his dad's whole rotten empire toppled and George with it. He wants closure or outright avoidance, to be able to pack his bags like he did years ago and walk away, but for good this time. He wants to kick Alex out of his head, or go out and find him, or do some dumb incriminating internet search to get his attention like a kid pulling pigtails, even though it might get Jack bumped up the shit list. On and on; these thoughts are just more cyclical futility, and he's wasting energy on them. His choices cost too much these days—or maybe they always have and Jack's only just realizing the weight of his debt for years of playing along.

More immediately Jack wants something to ease his headache. Some fresh air and a handful of painkillers, then. Simple enough.

On the street below a silver car pulls up as Jack fixes the window open a crack to let the breeze in. It's spattered with rain, but he's more focused on the car with its tinted windows, a figure in a black suit stepping out of the passenger side with a heavy coat pulled up to obscure his entire head.

The person from the phone call, maybe, and he quickly jogs up the path, Jack hearing the front door bang downstairs.

Jack swings open his own door, hanging back in the frame and trying to catch a glimpse of the man in the hall. He doesn't recognize this person, not like the judge, and Jack watches him stride up to his father's study, unbothered by Boyce, and let himself right in.

There are no raised voices this time and no chance for Jack to get closer with Boyce outside. And besides that, what would be the point? He's been hard-warned off his snooping, and as uneasily tempting as the possibility of another visit from Alex is, Jack's already walked away from pushing his luck enough times.

Except—

Seems like he's in a unique position here and precious gifts should never be squandered. His mom used to tell him that when she watched him draw.

Except—

What the fuck does he think he's doing, hovering at the event horizon of this rabbit hole all over again?

He shuts out the *maybes* and the *excepts* and the alarm bells ringing accusations, the headache digging roots and the unrelenting sense of his own heart beating in his chest. Right down until the only thing dictating him is logic: the consequences of his inaction versus the potential shit-storm of actually wading into a battle where the rules are blurry and the players unknown.

What if he could help?

If people are trying to kill his dad over whatever's going on out there in the war of law and politics, Jack can't sit on anything that could affect the outcome. He can't look in the other direction and pretend everything's going to be fine.

Not anymore.

Incrimination is surely better than death? If Jack could hold proof in his hand instead of pages and pages of conjecture, something to use as leverage, just maybe—

He plucks a plaid shirt with a little breast pocket from his drawer and tries putting his phone in it; the camera peeks ideally out over the top. That has to be a good sign, right?

He feels like a fucking Hardy Boy, but there's nothing for it— the second he hears his father's study door open, Jack presses Record, grabs a glass from his nightstand, positions his phone, and heads out into the hall.

His gait feels stiff, like his anxiety is on spectacular display, but he walks resolutely toward the suited man with a single disinterested look passing between them.

Jack veers right into the bathroom just before the stairs to run the sink tap hard, filling up his glass loud enough to maybe cover his ass. He takes a long drink of freezing water that lances through his head and makes his vision bleed vivid with sharp colors, and then he fills the glass again to take back to his room, water rippling by his trembling hand.

He shuts the door, sinking down onto the bed and fumbling with the phone to stop the video and play it back.

The image is shaky and a little dark from the hall lighting, but the man's face is on it, thick graying hair slicked back with pomade or rainwater, generic, doughy features.

Jack picks the clearest frame and takes a screen capture, brightening and sharpening until it's as defined as he can make it.

And now he has a choice, the novelty lying in that alone, more control over his situation than he's had in a good long while. That he could sit on this forever and remain safe, watch the chips fall as they may, is still a comfort, even though he knows he won't.

He runs through the various ways of using the picture, getting it out there, and settles on a brief appearance on his work Twitter, uploaded with the words *anyone know this man?* for fifteen heart-pounding minutes of sitting static on his bed before taking it down again. It won't mean much to his friends and acquaintances, but it will mean something to someone.

Jack's waved his white flag now. There's no going back.

For a second, he considers trying to sleep again, anything to shift this drumming ache in his head, but he's ticking over, brain in overdrive, a current skittering uncomfortably between his skin and muscle.

But the possibility becomes moot with a knock on his door.

Jack's heart fucking *lurches*. He's been caught, they figured him out, he was so damn obvious, how could he have been so *stupid*—

"Boyce," he says quietly. "What can I do for you?"

He's so rarely heard Boyce speak, and his voice is always oddly low and soft, kind of lulling. "Your father wants you."

"Right."

Jack stuffs his phone in his pocket and follows Boyce up the hall, getting let into the study under one of Boyce's huge arms.

Inside the room, his father's face is pinched and tight, stuck in a thoughtful frown, and Jack clears his throat, half to catch his wavering attention and half to get his own voice steady.

"What d'you want?" he asks.

"To talk about the new ground rules." George is distracted, and Jack's heart calms some, enough to understand he's in the clear but not enough to be completely safe.

"Who was your friend?" he asks in a thoughtless rush.

His dad turns sharply, perching on the edge of his desk.

"What?"

"Your friend, who's so important I gotta take a number for my own tongue lashing."

"A business associate, what is it to you?"

"All right." Jack puts his hands up. "Didn't mean to hit a nerve. I was just asking."

His father is suddenly on his feet again and coming at Jack with long strides across the carpet. He stops just short, shoulders squared and back straight, and Jack straightens up to equal height in response, feeling more on guard than he thinks he should.

"A nerve?" his father asks quietly. Jack just cannot read his expression at all. "Did you come in here to rile me up, Jack, is that it?"

"No, I came in here because you asked—"

"I ask a lot of things of you."

"And I do what I can," Jack tries, but his dad's eyes get wider, pupils swollen; he looks a little unhinged.

"Little out of character for you, son."

That *does* hit a nerve, and Jack feels his mouth twist. "You can't be serious. I'm *here*, aren't I? Pretending like the good son, doing your stupid fucking PR bidding."

"And why's that?" George's voice hits its lowest point. "You fight me on every little thing, but you never hesitate to come into my house when I need you."

"You know why," Jack mutters, teeth gritted.

"Because of your mother." His father barks a laugh. "She's your big excuse, right, Jack? Just like always." Jack moves, shouldering hard past his dad to get some distance and sending him staggering. "Looks like *I've* hit a nerve."

"What is your Goddamn problem?" Jack demands, his back to the window where Alex broke in. The rain strikes the glass like a hail of bullets; it's so dark it looks like evening. "You have an argument with your *associate* and now you're taking it out on me?"

"Did the promise you made her extend to not sticking a knife in my back?"

He stands numb for a second, trying to slur out the words, "You're paranoid."

"Someone tried to kill me."

"And I saved your life."

"How convenient."

"No," Jack breathes. "No fucking way. You can't possibly think I had anything to do with that." His dad narrows his eyes, no other movement apart from that. "You," Jack splutters. "Everything you do, all the people you screw over, and you seriously think *I'm* the reason someone wanted to murder you!"

"What, what do I do?" his dad asks, so quick and cutting Jack's hardly got his wits together.

"You bleed this city dry, bribing your way to the top to enforce bullshit laws to line your pockets while everybody else struggles."

The ball is rolling now; Jack's struggling to pull it back. "You've got judges on your payroll, for God's sake! And who else? Who just walked outta here on your dime? How far does it go, Dad?"

He's irreparably fucked it now, he thinks, but a shove off a sheer cliff is quite the decision maker. If Jack was looking for the motivation to plow forward, shake up the status quo, he's really brought it on himself. It's a lot of heights to fall from in one day, but Jack's never done things with much subtlety.

George stays silent, and Jack lets him, both of them breathing audibly to the backbeat of the rain. There's a palpable suspense in the room like the flip of a coin: which way is it gonna land?

"Those are some very serious accusations," is all his father says.

Jack holds his ground. "Tell me I'm wrong."

"And what do you intend to do with what you think you know?"

"No, that's not what I—" Jack scrubs a hand over his face, up through his hair. "I'm asking you what the hell you think you're doing here. Because all this shady crap is gonna get you killed."

It's not wholly the truth; Jack's phone burns in his pocket, an inescapable reality, but if his dad would just give him something, a show of remorse, a hint of humanity, *anything,* Jack could feel differently. He could extend that psychical act of saving his father's life all those nights back to something more than a deathbed promise made a decade ago.

His father hums, "Hmm." He purses his mouth, walking to his desk and pulling out a yellowing file and a checkbook. "How much?"

It takes a moment to sink in. "How—*much*. How much money will it take to pay me to shut up?"

"Cost of living isn't cheap these days, even the life you choose to lead. And it could be worse, still." He opens up the file, slipping out a piece of paper. "Your rent, for example."

It's a headed letter that's startlingly familiar, Jack's fake-name signature scratched across the bottom.

He feels numb.

"You can't possibly—"

"Own your apartment, that I expend every effort to keep affordable, yes."

"All this time," Jack breathes.

"Oh, don't be so naïve. Did you honestly think I'd trust you out there on your own?" George asks roughly. "Selling your *witty* art and making a public spectacle of yourself outside bars and, and nightclubs in the early hours of the morning, getting inappropriate with barmen in front of interns from the Review!"

And like a spotlight flooding a stage, Jack can see his life all lit up through his father's eyes. "How do you even—"

"Do you know how much it cost me to bury those pictures?" He waves the file as he talks. "Or the dozens of other stories that have landed on my desk over the years?"

"What the *hell*, Dad, you've been having me stalked?"

"Keeping an eye on you, and it's a good thing—"

"I've got nothing to hide! I'm not ashamed. I don't give a crap, Dad! The only person who cares about this stuff is you; the only person you are helping is *you*." He takes a breath. "I don't want your money. I never wanted anything from you."

His father's face smooths out into that careful arrangement of calm that Jack hates. "And yet here we are."

"You can't buy or own people."

"That's business, son."

Jack grits his teeth. "You can't own *me*."

"Maybe not with money, but money isn't the only way to trade. I don't endure threats, Jack."

"What?"

He is fast losing track of this conversation, cowed by his father's quick, volatile tongue.

"Especially not unsubstantiated ones made by a bitter child angry that he never made anything of himself." This version of his father, Jack knows well. Distant and cool, flatly spoken but full of implication. "You may be my son, but that doesn't mean I won't treat you like an enemy if I have to. You and anyone else you see fit to throw your lot in with."

Jack knows this version but never like this.

"Are you threatening me?" he asks weakly.

"You presume to have me all figured out—what do you think?"

Jack takes a breath, slow and minimally stuttering. "Clearly there's more to you than I realized."

"Don't make an enemy of me, son."

He looks, he really does, for anything in his father's face that suggests hesitation, an internal struggle of some sort over what's coming out of his mouth. Like it's not *that easy* for George Preston to have his own son scared into submission to protect himself.

But there's nothing, and it seems it is that easy. Jack never could've guessed his safety at the hands of his own parent could be up for question. The thought is just inconceivable.

He looks until he can't look anymore, glancing everywhere but and feeling defeated with his father's eyes still smug on him. The shelved books he used to stack like blocks as a kid, the desk lamp that burns abnormally hot, stacked files and letters, an access ticket of some kind with a signature way more elegant than Jack's own delicately curled across the bottom.

"Boyce."

Jack turns his head at the click of the door, and Boyce is hulking there.

His dad takes a step forward, gesturing. "Take Jack back to his room; make sure he doesn't leave it without me being informed."

"You can't do this," Jack tells his impassive father. "This is insane." Boyce grips his arm, tugging him firmly. "It's not just insane—it's illegal!"

"Take his phone, too."

He can feel his panicked stare trying to appeal. Boyce digs a rough hand through Jack's clothes regardless, pocketing his phone while Jack tries to shrug out of his grip, get away, *anything*; a pointless fight, but he's just fucking—reeling, he can't—

Boyce drags him into the hall, and Jack finds himself galvanized, funneling panic and anger into his body. He lurches half out of Boyce's hold, making a clumsy dash for the stairs, but Boyce is much faster than he looks for a guy his size, and Jack ends up with his arm twisted up his back, grabbing out for anything to hold on to as he gets hauled in the direction of his room.

His fingers close around a vase, and he throws it, watching it smash against his father's study door, before he's ceremoniously spun and thrown into his bedroom, where Boyce seals him in with a slam that shakes the frame.

Jack launches himself straight back against it like a snapping rubber band, rattling the handle and banging with his fists, his shoulder, until his bones feel bruised and his throat is scratchy.

Until very real dread hits him like a slap.

He staggers back and stares at the wood, jaw dropped, for so long his vision starts to swim and he has to sit down, put his head in his aching hands and collect himself.

He's—what? A prisoner now? A fucking prisoner in his own family home, where he flipped a skateboard down the hall floorboards and ate breakfast in his parents' bed on Saturday mornings and watched his mom slowly die—

"Oh, *God*," he breathes, swallows, a tremble building in him. "Can't be, can't be."

It *can't* be.

Jack stands up too soon, half-blind from the spots in front of his eyes, and stumbles to the window, flinging it open so hard it bounces on its hinges. The drop down is long and unbroken, nothing but concrete slabs and two broken legs to land on. The rain still comes, wetting the inside window ledge, spraying like mist against Jack's heated face.

He leans out into the wind, rapidly blinking droplets of water from his eyelashes and pulling desperate air into his body right out of the sky.

Chapter Nine

Five days pass in a numb crawl.

The first twelve hours he spends *calming down* in his room, sealed in by one of the PMCs at the door telling Jack how un-fucking-reasonable his yelling is.

After that Jack haunts the second floor of the house like a ghost for a while, not stepping foot beyond the top of the stairs where Boyce stands watching with his radio—or one of the others, when Jack's father leaves for the lodge in his nondescript black car under the cover of darkness.

The two times that he does, Jack heads downstairs to get ignored by the security—like they've been warned off making conversation with him now. He can't get near the doors and the windows are all sealed shut, bathroom exit included. Regina and Charlie are nowhere to be seen inside the house, but he catches Regina climbing into the surveillance van a couple times, looking grim and hurried.

Someone makes him regular meals. Someone also changes the Wi-Fi password. People sometimes come and go from the townhouse in tinted vehicles, their faces always covered. Jack loses interest in these things after a couple of days, the fight leeched out of him.

His existence becomes thin like cellophane; he forgets the sound of his own voice or how to want to use it. He sleeps fitfully, wading in and out of consciousness, never really going under, but mostly Jack just sits at his open bedroom window in a kind of detached disbelief, waiting for the other shoe to drop.

It stubbornly won't, but that doesn't mean the feeling is easy to shake.

In his worst moments, Jack wonders why he didn't just stand aside and let Alex kill his father. But the thought spreads like a disease, evolves or, or *devolves* into the ache of longing for the guy he walked away from only last week. All the wildest, most cliché daydreams: if Alex knew what was happening right now, would he ride in here and free Jack? Would he care?

Those are hard to shake, too. Harder because he actually believes in it so utterly, like if he could just get some kind of message out of this place then Alex would help him. It becomes a thought caught in a web, so deeply woven and sticky he can't shift it.

But beyond putting up SOS signs in his window and praying he's not delusional, Jack thinks he's pretty screwed. Imprisoned here forever for some unspecified reason and until some unspecific moment in time. His dad's given no instruction, no demand, and that's the worst part, being left to figure out the whims of a madman like this.

Maybe he caves in and lets his father groom him into an acceptable son, or relents and takes the money and disappears to another state somewhere. Or worse—he's quietly offed. He hasn't discounted the uncomfortable possibility of that being on the table.

The alternative could be Jack and everyone around him ruined, chewed up and tossed out with nothing, because his dad has untold legions of powerful people at his disposal and how can Jack hope to fight that?

He's too close to drowning in despondency; it's probably what his dad was counting on.

He stares down at the early morning sidewalk, watching Mrs. Mosley walk her dog across the street and between the park gates. Some kind of poodle mix, he thinks idly. A poodle with a lab, maybe.

The sun keeps flashing through the broken clouds, dark then light then dark again. It's breezy, but it's always breezy. Jack flips his sketchpad to portrait and tries to draw the rows of sugar maples from memory, convinced that if he can create something today he can pull himself together a little tighter.

The shaded path splits the two maple rows down the middle. The branch-lines and little leaf-shape outlines come next. He colors the background with the flat of his graphite, so it's night, and the streetlamps spot white through it. With the point of his pencil, he makes a tiny figure appear under one of the maples and then colors over it, feeling ridiculous.

He supposes ridiculous is better than hopeless. Hope sees him figuring out how to bust through a thick-glass window and making a dive for it, hoping it causes enough commotion that he can either get away or alert the authorities.

If the authorities aren't also on his father's payroll.

By the time he's finished overdoing the details of the picture, the sun is really shining. He cracks the window, breathing in the smell of ozone and rain drying from the nighttime deluge, holding out a hand to let the light sit in his palm.

He spots Mrs. Mosley's dog through his curled fingers, yapping back and forth by the park gate, and Jack folds his arms on the ledge to watch it run circles around itself until Mrs. Mosley trails wearily up behind it.

Jack's been doing this a lot, the people watching thing. His grandparents used to own an apartment overlooking a meadow and every day they'd put on the TV but watch the kids playing sports and the dog walkers instead. They were living vicariously, he thinks, because his grandparents couldn't get out much in their old age. He's always been a people watcher, but now he understands his impulse: being in a cage means you're always looking out, and Jack's been in a cage his whole life, even when he didn't or couldn't acknowledge it.

He watches Mrs. Mosley stoop down with some difficulty to

leash her dog, a thing she's always done to cross the street even though the street's about eight feet wide and sees half a dozen cars an hour at best. Jack doesn't know if it's his imagination in overdrive, but she looks concerned about something, and when she stalls at the curb for several minutes, he finds he's trying and failing, over and over, to hold his breath.

She looks up—up at his window, up, up right into his damn face, *up*.

Jack startles, blinking, and slowly raises a hand to give her a little wave. She returns it, face still drawn tight into a frown, and he sees her hesitate before she points right at him with her finger, curling her whole hand into the symbol for *OK* right afterwards.

She's asking if he's okay?

Thoughtlessly, he shakes his head, and he's dizzy with how fast his blood starts to rush, the speed and intensity of his heart all of a sudden. Mrs. Mosley's eyebrows climb into her wispy hair line, shock slackening her features into a gape, and then she's turning away from him, pulling the dog back into the park with a far greater speed than she left it.

He watches after her helplessly, heart lodged up in his throat, and then he leans out of the open window, checking the surveillance van down the street for any sign of trouble.

Nothing.

Nothing, and Jack might have imagined all of that, mind inflamed from being forcibly confined indoors and living on the very edge of his nerves.

Mrs. Mosley's notoriously quirky, walks her dog through blizzards and rearranges furniture at three AM, and the van never moved, nobody got out to follow her. Every bit of logic Jack possesses tells him—

The shrill and sudden whine of the fire alarm puts an end to *that*, and Jack jumps up from the window seat and over to the door, swinging it open and spotting one of the other guys and not Boyce in the hall.

"What the hell is going on?"

"Sir, you better come with me."

"Where's my dad?"

The man tenses a second, flitting a look between Jack and the blaring alarm. "Still out, sir, now come with me."

And like that, Jack can smell smoke. "There's an actual fucking fire?"

He hurries to the security guy's side, getting ushered down the stairs and into the hall while the man speaks into the crackle of his radio. "Fire at the premises; I need a car ASAP."

Jack's shaking in front of the open front door, shoved through it and quickly overwhelmed by the miles of sky and feel of concrete under his shoes. "What do you mean he's still out?"

"Pulled an all-nighter," the man—Wade, Jack remembers— tells him distractedly, watching one of his companions, weapon surreptitiously drawn, scouting the outside of the townhouse while he keeps one protective hand on Jack's shoulder.

Charlie dashes over to them from the gate, and Jack's struck by the sight of his rueful half smile greeting when it feels like forever since he saw a friendly face. "Fire's at the back, whole garden is up in flames, and it's gonna spread inside and *soon*."

"How did the entire garden set on fire?" Jack asks, because there's no way this is a coincidence. Wade doesn't seem to think so either, glaring down at him. "Hey, it wasn't me! I wasn't anywhere near the back door—you should all know that well enough."

Charlie ignores Wade, telling Jack, "It looks and smells like an accelerant was used."

"Another assassination attempt?"

"A pretty lame one," Charlie sighs and then turns at the sound of fire sirens fading in. "Your dad isn't even here." He gives Jack a pat on the arm before he leaves them, tells him, "Stay with Wade, kid."

A black car pulls up right behind a fire truck, and in the frantic hustle of people moving to and fro, Jack doesn't see Mrs. Mosley and her dog lurking by the park gate until he's already been herded into the vehicle with the automatic locks clicked down. He twists in his seat, desperately trying to get a look at her, but the driver pulls away from the curb, and they're speeding down the road before he can.

"What? What it is?" Wade asks, sitting tense beside him, and

Jack shakes his head.

"Nothing."

"If you saw something—"

"My elderly neighbor. She's probably wondering why her street's on fucking fire."

He stares resolutely out the window, grounding himself with every breath, feeling inescapably caught in some colossal, ominous tide.

"Where are you taking me?"

"Somewhere safe."

They make a right turn onto a quiet road, and Jack really doesn't feel all that safe. "Somewhere I can be locked up again?"

"Not my decision, sir."

Jack huffs a humorless, "Sir," as the car screeches to an abrupt halt. His chest crushes against the seatbelt, hands coming up to butt against the front seat, and he's more than a little winded, disorientated from the brake-skid lurching the car horizontal across the road.

Something hard cracks against the driver window, makes the glass splinter outward like a web, and the driver's unconscious from the crash, Jack realizes, slumped against the steering wheel and barely moving. Both PMCs' radios bounce white noise back and forth over a voice demanding a report, and the crack at the window happens again and again, car metal groaning and engine steaming; a whole orchestra of terror.

Jack can't breathe, scrabbling for his seatbelt clip while Wade positions himself to train his gun on the window.

"Stay down," he tells Jack, and Jack presses back into his seat as much as he can without being able to phase through solid matter. "Cover your ears."

Crack and the window shatters, safety glass crumbling in and an arm reaching for the keys. Jack cups his hands over his ears as Wade's bullet slams right through the remaining glass and at whoever's outside.

"Son of a—"

Jack looks at Wade, squinting through the dust and palpable sound of ringing in his head, and for a second he thinks that's it, it's gotta be over.

Then several things happen at once, so fast, so fucking dazzling, that he can't track which comes first. The automatic locks buzz open, a small bullet wound makes a visceral mess of Wade's shoulder, and someone grabs the back of Jack's sweater.

He's hauled, staggering, out of the car by the scruff of his neck, and then guided away, up onto the sidewalk and down a little alleyway, and he'd go anywhere right now, the waning and paranoid state he's in—shaking to his bones and numbed from there up. Death feels like it's waiting at the end of this forced march, the tide drawing him quickly to it, if he could just—just remember how to fight—

He's moving quickly down the alley, surrounded on both sides by high buildings, can't place where he is. The hand holding him, guiding him, slips away and footsteps echo up the walls, against the fire escapes, the scratched and greenish dumpsters.

Jack shuts his eyes, turns his face up to the sun.

"Jack," a very faint, far-off voice says, and Jack looks down, can't fucking *see* what he's seeing.

He breaks down the distance between them unsteadily, colliding with a body—Alex's body.

"Hey, hey, it's okay," Alex soothes, and Jack grips his sides with weak fingers, pressing his face into Alex's throat. "Jack, it's okay, but we have to keep moving."

"This is—" he chokes out. "This is *not* okay."

A pause, a hand curling briefly at the back of his neck, and then: "Okay, it's not okay, but we still gotta move."

A voice calls urgently from somewhere behind him, Alex's name, female speaker, and Alex grips Jack's wrist and tugs him into motion in the opposite direction, all the way through the alley until they hit the parallel street under the full glow of the mid-morning sun that Jack was certain he was going to die under.

He lets Alex keep a hold of him, feels like he's siphoning off some of Jack's terrified energy and putting it to good use. "Who was that?"

"A colleague, telling me to get my ass moving."

He knows where they are now: the cobbled paths and massive sand-blasted factory buildings of Little Germany. Alex must've picked up the security car coming down St. Cecilia street, heading into one of the oldest parts of the city.

"Where are you taking me?" he asks, second time today caught in a drift. It doesn't sound right at all, and he rephrases: "Where are we going?"

"Somewhere safe," Alex tells him softly, thumb firm over Jack's pulse-point, and this time he damn well believes it.

Alex leads him into and through the crowded shopping avenue, past the red-and-white awning of the Suben Café where Jack's memories are vivid and cutting, and into an arch between two buildings.

He directs them again through the back alleys, until they reach a fire escape stark against a graffiti-covered wall, where he urges Jack up the groaning metal steps. A whole lifetime ago they did a thing just like this; three times is a pattern.

He must've said that out loud and Alex tells him, "But twice is a coincidence."

"You got one more to go, then."

His voice is wavering as he hits the roof in a glare of light, turning to watch Alex climb up after him.

He's hesitant against Jack's attention, running a hand through his hair. Jack wants to stop looking so they can move, he does, but Alex is a miracle right off the page of a book, and Jack went through all of the motions, thought he'd never see him again, tried to attract his attention, waited for a fairytale rescue, mourned and yearned in equal measure.

"C'mon, it's the next building over."

Jack looks where Alex is gesturing. "That's the playhouse."

"My buddy owns the apartment over it."

Alex waits for him to nod his consent before taking off again.

The playhouse roof is lower than this one, and they drop down and then down again onto a back balcony overlooking the narrow alley. The door to the inside is cracked open a little, and Alex pushes his elbow into the tiny gap and jimmies it all the way, stepping aside to let Jack in first.

He shuts it behind them, sunlight filtering through the dust in speckled streams, and with the gentle click, the sense of finality feels like a valve releasing pressure, the ability to breathe freely a revelation.

He ducks his head and sighs, and thinks he might be wearing that sentiment all over his face.

"Hey," Alex says softly, meaningless and yet—

Jack swallows, sighs a laugh.

Alex goes on, shrugging off his dark jacket and the gun holster concealed underneath and laying them both over the back of a sofa. "You'll be safe here, not even the—nobody knows about this place."

Jack finishes the aborted statement for him. "Not even the people you work for?" And Alex nods, a barely perceptible jerk of his head. "How suspicious."

Alex smirks. It's different from before, though, from their little nighttime furlough from sanity. In fact, now that Jack really looks, *Alex* is different from before, the whole sum of his parts less somehow; less bold, less otherworldly, less untouchable. He's casual in the bright light of day, hands stuffed in the pockets of his jeans and his bare forearms lean and vulnerable—a fallacy, Jack knows, because Alex is anything but vulnerable. But knowing that doesn't stop the warm thread of want winding itself into his bloodstream.

He's also keeping a careful distance, physically and not so, like Jack might back away from him again.

"It's a friend's place," Alex explains, and then pointlessly adds, "A friend and his sister's."

"So, a safe house?" Jack guesses.

"Unofficial, but safe."

Safe; that word again. He shudders, Wade's voice telling him the same damn thing, his blood, his blood on the back window—

"Wade?" Jack asks, voice quiet because his head is miles back now with the smell of leaking diesel and the tortured groan of smashed metal.

"Your PMC? Shot, but alive. The driver's gonna be fine, too."

Jack exhales slowly, wants to ask why, why spare their lives? But the relief is the final straw that cripples him. "And—and Mrs. Mosley, my dad—"

"We don't have to do this now."

"*Is my dad alive?*"

"Yes, your father is alive. He spent all night at the lodge." Jack shuts his eyes, no clue how to feel about that. "Your neighbor's fine, too. She was concerned about some activity at the house, and she called the cops today and was intercepted. I asked her to help me out. Jack, what the hell happened?"

Jack shakes his head. "We had a disagreement."

"You uploaded a photograph of Jacob Kalhoff to your Twitter account."

"Jacob Kalhoff."

"A very influential stock broker who recently went to trial for a lotta bad crap."

And a heavy campaigner for his father's team years ago, Jack remembers. Right up until Kalhoff went under very public investigation.

"He was meeting my dad at the house. They all come to the house now," Jack tells him, adding, "Since you tried to shoot him, he's been too scared to go out much."

Alex nods slowly; looks like he already knew that. "After the picture I, uh, hoped to get a hold of you, but no luck."

"Tell me about it."

"Did your father find out?"

"No," Jack assures him. "I went off at him for being corrupt as hell, and he threatened me and locked me up."

Alex's expression animates like a live wire; Jack recognizes it from before, Alex telling him that *someone* had to stop his father. "Fucking—" he mutters, and then he snaps out of it. "What the hell were you thinking?"

"I was thinking," Jack starts acerbically, "that he's my dad, and generally, dads don't do shit like that to their kids."

"And taking the picture?"

"I mean—my dad got this guy off, right? Another bribery, another acquittal? Seems to me like it could be pretty convincing evidence."

"At the cost, *again,* of your safety—"

Jack steps away, puts his hand on the wall for balance. He is so, *so* tired. "Didn't cost me shit, it was fine, and why do you care anyway?"

He regrets it as soon as it comes out of his mouth, but not because it isn't a good question; it is. Alex's whole overprotective shtick is as wildly unfathomable as Jack's implicit trust in him, but Jack feels like he's hinged to it now, like it and the wall are the only things keeping him upright.

"I was sent out to pick you up today," Alex says expressionlessly.

"Just the job, then." Jack does not believe that. He delivers it like a challenge, Alex's mouth a grim line. "Who was that woman? You said she was covering your ass."

"Someone I work with."

"You—" Jack swallows hard, turning to lean his back against

the wall. "You have to give me *something*, Alex! I'm in the wind here, and I hate it. It's driving me crazy."

"I was supposed to pick you up and deliver you," Alex blurts out, pinching his bottom lip like he's trying to collect the words and put them back. "But I didn't. I brought you here instead."

"Deliver me where?"

"To my handlers."

Jack tips his head back, last piece of the puzzle settling wearily into place. "You're government, aren't you?"

He doesn't need Alex to answer, but he does anyway. "Yeah."

"A spook."

"Something like that."

"That's an arm I can't outrun." Jack closes his eyes, sighing deep. "I was still kinda holding out for a paid hit-job."

"Sorry to disappoint."

Jack laughs, can't decide whether it's actually funny or not. "I don't think I have it in me to be disappointed by you."

It's a highly candid admission, unplanned, but Jack doesn't regret this one at least. Alex tells him, "You haven't known me long enough," but he sounds breathless, and Jack doesn't open his eyes, stupidly afraid that Alex's expression won't look like the version currently sitting pretty in his imagination.

"And yet here we are."

"Jack."

Fuck, he wasn't nearly prepared for that; Alex closer now,

begging Jack's name in a voice that's hoarse. Jack's not exactly sure what he just admitted to, but he aches with it, all his skin tender.

He opens his eyes, says simply, "Alex."

"You should lie down, you're dead on your feet," Alex says gently.

"I don't—"

Alex interrupts him. "I'll be here when you wake up." Because of course he knew, of *course* he did. "And no offense, but you look like you haven't slept in like a week."

Jack snorts. "Thanks."

"There's a bedroom down the hall, at the end, and the bathroom's on the right."

Jack takes a look around properly for the first time since they landed here. The little lounge is sparse: two sofas covered with white sheets, a low rectangular wooden coffee table, a television tucked into one corner, and a wall rowed with shelves full of dusty looking books. The walls are pale blue, the room bright and airy despite its size, and there's a doorway leading into the kitchen along the farthest wall.

Jack navigates his way through the furniture and to the bathroom.

The light from outside comes in crisscrossing beams through latticed window shutters, catching on the mosaic blue-green tiles, and a gaudy boucherouite rug slips under his shoes, curled up at the edges for the lack of anything to stick it to the floor. Jack runs a brass tap until the water is freezing, scooping up handfuls to drench his face, and the mirror above the sink framed in stained glass fragments shows him his appalling reflection.

Alex wasn't wrong.

He finds the bedroom at the end of the hall, decorated like the living room—these friends of Alex's sure like their color scheme—with a creamy carpet and blue walls, white bed linen and curtains.

He takes off his shoes and sweater and crawls into the middle of the double bed, positive the throb behind his eyes and the adrenaline of the chase is going to make sleeping impossible.

And then he promptly goes under with all the grace of a lead weight.

Chapter Ten

He's dreaming in yellows and grays.

A sickly, monochrome world and the hard sounds of something huge, something rolling toward him. Coming for him.

He's choking. His mouth is full of dust, paper, cotton—

Jack drags his face out of the pillow, breathing hard. The images in his head are flickering fuzz like static, graying out before he has the foresight to try to commit to them, and he rolls his forehead against his folded arm, the murky feeling smoothing out as he realizes where he is.

It's getting dark outside, the tail end of the sun setting maybe, and tinged with a yellow-orange haze that he thinks, for a foggy second, is more fire.

Then the thunder sounds somewhere close.

Jack rolls out of bed, scrubbing his eyes with an open palm. There are no clocks in this room and his phone's long since been kidnapped so he gets up, navigating the windowless hall in the dark with his hand brushing against the walls.

The apartment is quiet except for the unmistakable sound of wind, and he follows the feel of it into the lounge, where the screen door is cracked open.

Jack freezes, fighting with himself and his fucked-up adrenal response over the familiar figure outside that's obviously Alex.

He's standing with his back to Jack, elbows against the balcony rail, and Jack clears his throat softly enough to get his attention without startling him, making him turn and tip his chin in a greeting.

Jack joins him, air swollen with clouds and lightning, the whole sky above them a vast gunmetal-gray unrest but the area far beyond all rimmed in pink and silver, still faintly light. He looks at Alex, his complexion under this sunset storm, and thinks coming out here might have been a bad idea; all sorts of ways this could go, the end of a tether a pretty reckless place to be.

There's no rain yet, and out here, it smells metallic, charged and ozoney. Jack's thin T-shirt sticks to him and he feels like he's suffocating.

"Sleep okay?" Alex asks.

"Yeah, surprisingly." He mirrors Alex, leaning against the rail. "Messed up, though." He dips his head, alley below them empty. "Whole sleep schedule's screwed now."

Alex huffs. "I haven't had a sleep schedule in years."

"What time is it?" It's thoughtless; his fingers circle Alex's wrist, delicate pulse fluttering into his fingertips. He leans over, barely inches, to check Alex's watch. It's almost nine. "Too early for bedtime yet," he softly quips. "I wouldn't worry too much."

Alex makes a fist, tendons and bones shifting in the palm of Jack's hand. "Wonderful. Where were you all my life?"

"Staying out of it," Jack mutters, amused, and Alex chuckles.

"Nothing good ever lasts forever."

"Isn't that a song?"

Alex takes his hand back slowly; Jack just hadn't had the good sense to let him go. "You're thinking of Tears for Fears."

"Or Lorde."

Alex laughs again, and it does nothing to clear the dreamlike lushness of Jack's muzzy head. "Everybody Wants to Rule the World."

"Appropriate, huh?"

"You're a struggling artist," Alex points out fairly.

Jack slants him a sideways look. "And you're a government assassin."

"I prefer Special Operations myself."

There's a silence Jack thinks he's supposed to fill, but he's too fascinated with the uncomfortable expression over Alex's profile—the dip of his throat and the shape of his pursed mouth.

"Do you hate it?" he asks.

Alex shrugs. "It's a job."

"It's not your average job." It's easier in this half light to ask, "How do you even get into something like that?"

"I was," Alex says, hesitating, "recruited."

"If you told me, would you have to kill me?"

Alex groans. "If I had a dollar for every time someone's made that joke at me."

"I'm tired, give me a break."

"Nah, man, I rescued you, I expect top-quality humor as repayment."

"Rescued," Jack huffs. "God, would you believe I'd almost forgotten about this clusterfuck of a day?"

Alex nudges him, shoulder to shoulder. "I'm sorry." They've done this before, Jack knows; a balcony, a theatre, a night sky.

"You know, I'd almost pegged you for a theatre kid," Jack says slyly, and Alex shakes his head, grinning.

"I dabbled."

"Theatre kid, all-star athlete, God, were you the inspiration for that guy from High School Musical?"

"Zac Efron *wishes* he had talent like mine."

Jack glances him up and down. "I don't doubt that."

Alex blinks at him, half-lidded and slow, and Jack looks away, back up at the apocalyptic sky as the thunder rolls, sounds like it can't get much closer now.

His fingers feel sluggish when he curls his hands into loose fists, squirming warmth in his belly weakening him. "Where was I supposed to be today? Instead of here?"

"Detained and questioned, somewhere off the grid."

"Wow," Jack breathes. "Like a suspect?"

"To begin with, and once they'd decided how loyal you were to your father, however long that took, they'd wanna know how useful you could be."

"And if I couldn't?"

"I don't know," Alex hedges, like maybe he does but doesn't want to talk about it. "But it's why I came to you and asked you to stop snooping."

"Which I didn't."

"Which you didn't," Alex repeats pointedly. "Why'd you upload the picture?"

Jack shrugs, but he answers anyway, compelled to explain himself. "Because my dad's the bad guy. Because I realized my doing nothing was making me complicit."

"Not in the eyes of the law."

"No," Jack agrees. "But it was getting harder to live with myself. Can't stick your head in the sand forever, right?"

"You can when it keeps you safe."

"I'm safe now." Jack turns his hip against the railing, watching Alex head-on. "You said." Alex watches the alleyway blankly. "Rescued, I think, was the *exact* the word you used," Jack tries, pushing. "Obviously the next step is going on the run together, fake passports, new identities, hunted to the ends of the earth—"

"*All right,*" Alex breaks. "Ever considered a career interrogating prisoners?" Jack raises his eyebrows expectantly. "They'll expect me to bring you in."

"*What?*"

"I kinda took off with you. I might get forty-eight hours leeway on the subject because David—because I'm trusted."

"Forty-eight hours to do what?"

"I didn't want you to be any part of this," Alex stresses. "I know you're completely innocent, Jack, and you don't deserve to be threatened or used."

Jack—he ignores that, has to, and takes a stab in the dark: "Forty-eight hours to make me an asset, to turn me and make me useful." And when Alex nods, he asks, "Can *you* do that, officially?"

"Right now I think it's the only thing I can do for you."

Yeah, Jack understands now. He's understood, on some level, since he recorded a shaky video of Jacob Kalhoff in the hall. He's backed himself into this corner eagerly, given himself no excuses to wriggle out of it.

"Okay," Jack says hoarsely. "I mean, I sure as hell won't be welcomed back home with open arms so I don't know how useful I can even be, but I'll try."

Alex considers him, meltingly soft. "I have to convince my handlers first."

"Go right ahead. I'll give them whatever I can."

"You're nuts."

Jack huffs a shaky laugh. "You're relying on me to bring down my father's fortress. I'd say we're even."

"It's not gonna be easy," Alex explains, like Jack doesn't

already know this vividly. "People talk, they rat him out by the dozens, but in the end they've got no evidence or they clam up."

"That why he had to die?"

Alex lights up like he's got a fuse running through him, a strength in his voice that's pure conviction, real and true belief. "He's trading killers out onto the streets, drug lords, corrupt bankers, human traffickers, child molesters, anyone with enough money or power to pay for their freedom. They walk out of the court houses, and he shuffles them into positions of influence and nobody can do a *damn* thing about it."

Shit.

Killers, traffickers, molesters; it hadn't occurred to Jack this was bigger than his father's many well-heeled friends patting each other's backs, gaining favors, endlessly desiring the alpha spot. His father's campaign for office and all the perks that came with it.

Jack's mouth is dry. "How?"

"Money, obviously, and we think secrets, too. You know the fraternity?" Alex asks, obviously meaning the highly prestigious lodge Jack's father has been a member of since after his mom died. "Lotta powerful men with shady appetites are members there, and your father is a meticulous record keeper."

He thinks of the manila file with his name on it. "I believe it. He used a similar tactic to threaten me."

"Well there you go," Alex marvels, giving Jack a small smile.

"You're useful already."

"So there is proof."

"I told you, he's meticulous. It's just a theory, *was* just a theory, but nobody's ever held evidence in their hands. If he keeps his blackmail material on record, I didn't know anyone close enough to find out where."

"Well, damn." Jack cocks his head, fake confidence lending itself to a smile of his own. "Your agency ever think about trying to recruit me before all this?"

Alex pulls a droll face. "Sure we did, Mata Hari, but you were high on the risk assessment." And then carefully, slowly, he explains, "It was felt by some that you had a strong sense of loyalty to your father."

"But not to you," Jack muses. "I *bugged you on paper*."

Alex grins. "You did."

"How about now?"

"I got you all worked out, Mr. Preston."

"Happy with the result?"

The first patters of rain finally hit Jack's bare forearm, thunder sounding right over them. They look up, synchronized, and watch the lightning crisscross wildly through the cloud layers. The colors of the sky run like ink, the very air tinted like a lens filter. Jack gets rainwater in his eyes and splutters a laugh, squinting down at Alex.

It starts to pour.

Alex leads them quickly inside, T-shirt starting to soak and stick to him, mold to the curve at the base of his spine. Jack reaches out carelessly, puts both hands there; spread fingers curling to the shape of Alex's hips and thumbs digging into the dimples he can feel just above Alex's waistband.

He stands with his back to the open screen door, to the beaded sound of rain and the quick flashes of lightning, with Alex so still against the press of his hands that he can't possibly be breathing. Jack's fingertips start looking for skin, he has to—has to tug up the T-shirt hem, run his unsteady knuckles over those little indentations that fit under his thumb so nicely.

Alex's skin pricks up into gooseflesh, and Jack *feels* it, chases it with the backs of his fingers.

"This isn't part of the recruiting process," Alex says, voice already hoarse. "Just so you know."

Jack takes a half step forward, just short of pressing them together completely. He takes a gentle hold of Alex's hips, dipping his head, burying his nose into Alex's hair. "Clearly I've seen too many movies."

"I mean it—you don't owe me anything."

Jack swallows, nosing down to the hairline at the back of Alex's neck. "You think I'm doing this because I owe you?"

Alex tips his head forward and sighs, a short moan breaking through the breath, and Jack rubs his dry, closed mouth against the first notch of Alex's spine, navigates his shaking hands under

Alex's T-shirt. His fingers spread across skin taut over lean muscles, and Alex shifts back into Jack.

The shock of it is debilitating; he's wanted this so fiercely over such a terrible period of time that it sucks all the air out of him, makes him weak-kneed.

Thunder rolls like the smash of his heart against Alex's back. Alex's stomach twitches under the flat of his palms. It's getting darker, the rain's like artillery fire, and the air's heavy on his damp skin, pressure cranked all the way unbearably up.

"Tell me it's okay," he says, restless fingers rhythmically stroking.

"Tell me why."

"'Cause I am so crazy," Jack groans, feels Alex trying to move and holds him tighter. "I am so crazy over you."

Alex is all motion, then; hands covering Jack's to slip his T-shirt over his head, pressing Jack's palms into his freshly exposed skin—God, Jack grips a shoulder and spins him, looks at him, his lean chest and stomach, the cut of his collarbones.

Alex smiles—no, it couldn't be called a smile, way too filthy for a smile. Jack stretches to full height, towering inches over him, walking him and that damned smile back against the wall without even touching. Alex's head tips back.

He's got Alex pinned with a look, goading Jack with that expression. It's like the night he broke in all over again, potential for ruin written all fucking over him.

Jack lifts a hand all the way up, runs it into Alex's hair and grips, angling him just right. He leans down, parts his mouth above Alex's, breathing in the air he exhales.

"Tell *me* why," Jack demands.

"You fascinate me," Alex murmurs. "I must be crazy too."

He's rapidly overwhelmed by that, crowding all the way close, hand not buried in dark hair flat on the wall beside Alex's head. Pressed together like this, Alex's legs spreading so accommodatingly, he can feel the throb of blood to his dick and the way Alex is getting hard against him.

Alex finally—*finally*—touches him. Warm hands climb up the back of his T-shirt, blunt nails either side of his spine. Jack crushes Alex into the wall, bending a knee to push his thigh hard against the shape of Alex's cock, give him something to grind down on as he palms the back of Alex's head and kisses him.

Alex parts right open for him, no hesitation, no pretension. Just letting Jack's tongue slip in between his lips, slick against his own, wet and dizzying. Jack's got him trapped all ways, boxed in and pinned on his thigh. He swallows needy noises from the back of Alex's throat, feels molded by Alex's fingers digging in his back.

He breaks away for the urgent shove of Alex's hands against his shirt, tears the thing over his head and tosses it somewhere and gets right back into Alex's swollen mouth, gets skin on skin, sticky from the oppressive air and the sweat.

He hooks a hand under one of Alex's thighs for leverage,

opening him some more for the stunning friction against his cock, grinding Alex down when he arches up.

Jack's not even sure they're gonna get horizontal because this feels way too good to stop, and he's wanted so long. Because all he wants to do is feel Alex like this; Jack's government killer reduced to a writhing mess against the wall.

He tears his mouth away to tip their foreheads together. He can't get air in his lungs. Alex turns his face into Jack's wrist, breathing damply there, soft smush of his mouth against Jack's blue veins hypnotic. Jack's fingers scrape rough across his jaw, Alex's mouth in his palm and then two fingers caught against Alex's bottom lip for just a second, a heart-lurching second, before he eagerly sucks them down.

Jack watches with his own mouth falling open, crooking his fingers against Alex's tongue, rubbing his fingertips into the back of a fluttering throat.

Jack's brain gets confused, mixes up the sensations. He's never witnessed a thing so crazy-hot—all Alex and how he's got Jack's head quite spectacularly in knots. His hand is spit-wet, slippery, and Jack tears it free, frantic by how Alex hikes his knee over Jack's hip to spread himself wider for it.

He fumbles open Alex's jeans, gets his hand inside, naked skin of Alex's cock against the heel of his palm that he revels in for a second. He presses lower, under Alex's balls, running a fingertip into the crease of his ass and over his hole.

God, he's tight. Jack's trembling with the push of his finger, feeling undone by it himself. Alex's own spit is barely enough to ease up the friction, but Jack's fucked if Alex even seems to care, arching into it, insistent.

He's murmuring, "C'mon, Jack, feels so fuckin' good," until Jack's fucking him open with two fingers and breathing hard, buried all the way up to his knuckles in the insane heat of him. Alex is entirely hard against Jack's wrist, leaking smears of pre-come into his skin every time Jack fingers his prostate, and his head tips back against the wall, riding it out, weak hands fisting in Jack's hair, touching his shoulders.

"You could get off like this, couldn't you?" Jack asks, smears it deliriously against Alex's mouth. "Oh my God, you could." Alex hums, teeth sunk in his lip. "You gonna let me fuck you?"

Alex nods against him, and Jack hauls him off his feet. They stagger back, Jack landing on the sofa with Alex in his lap and laughing, eyes lit up in the dark.

He puts up a hand—"Hold up"—and leans back, Jack hooking an arm around his waist to stop him tumbling to the floor.

"What're you doing?"

Alex opens a drawer in the coffee table, making a commotion for a second before pulling himself back up with a condom pinched between his fingers.

He grins.

Jack grins back, hands on Alex's hips to push him up his knees in the sofa cushions, straddling Jack's thighs. The position's too impossible to get Alex's jeans all the way off, but he gets them down, Alex's flushed dick right there. Jack catches the head on his tongue, putting a hand to Alex's mouth for him to slick up with more spit.

His fingers slip right back in and Alex chokes, "Oh, God, that's what you're—" and doesn't finish that sentence, Jack closing his mouth over the first couple inches of his cock, cutting him off completely.

Alex's hand presses into Jack's shoulder for balance, the other in his hair. The helpless curve of his body over Jack blocks out most of the light from the storm. He feels out Alex's prostate with his fingertips and stays on it, running the flat of his tongue against the underside of Alex's cock to catch the spurts of pre-come, denying him the friction he needs to get off until he's whimpering restlessly, held still by Jack's hand on his hip.

Jack sucks a sloppy kiss against the head, looking up with his fingers still all the way buried. "How's it feel?"

Alex blinks down at him, breathing erratically. "So—*so* good."

"I'm gonna make you come like this," Jack tells him roughly, his own cock throbbing painfully in his underwear, so much heat curling in his stomach he's writhing with it. "Keep my fingers right there." He twitches them, rubs hard while Alex moans. "And suck on your dick." He licks at the head of Alex's cock again. "Until you come down my throat."

"You keep talkin' like that, *God*," Alex grits out, and Jack grins up at him.

"And then I'm gonna come in your ass."

"Oh, fuck."

He catches Alex's cock between his lips again and sucks him as far down as the awkward angle lets him. He nails Alex with his fingers, strokes him with his tongue; it takes half a minute, he thinks, until Alex is whimpering and gasping, fisting his hand tight in Jack's hair and coming with a cry.

Alex shivers his way through it. He makes the most extraordinary noises. Jack's neck aches, but he keeps on him until he's wrung all the way out, crumpling down into Jack's lap with his head lolling right in the middle of Jack's chest.

"Jesus," he says, "Christ."

Jack realizes what Alex is doing when he hears the condom packet open up. Just the blind sensation of Alex's fingers rolling on the rubber, spitting and slicking him up, makes his balls tight.

He's not even gonna last thirty seconds at this rate.

Alex somehow kicks off his jeans without even moving away all that much. He grips Jack's cock tight, raises up on his knees and stretches himself around it.

"Fuck," Jack whispers, "fuck, you're—" He has no idea what he's trying to say, something ridiculous and embarrassing no doubt, but Alex grinds his hips, tipping his head back, and Jack can't *think* past the sight of this, the tight friction swallowing up his dick.

Alex is holding him so fucking deep, keeping Jack all the way inside him with short rolls of his hips, and it's better than what Jack imagined, fucking him long and hard. Alex holds the back of Jack's neck, kisses him vague and sloppy, and drowns him in intimacy.

Pressure builds steadily in his balls until he's gasping, arching his back to slide both arms around Alex's middle. He buries his face into Alex's throat and loses it, helplessly letting Alex milk the come out of him until he's spent and gripping him to stop.

It's only when the silence hits that he realizes he's been muttering Alex's name.

"You know," Alex starts breathily, "I really hope no one's watching this place."

Jack snorts a laugh into his skin, bitten, it feels like, by Jack's thoughtless mouth. "Better hope there's none of your little spy drones about, huh?"

"That'd be one hell of a return to work."

It's fully dark out now. The rain still lashes against the balcony tiles, soaking the carpet in the open screen doorway. The thunder is still sounding somewhere overhead, breeze of whipped-up atmosphere slipping its way inside to cool the stifling room.

Jack runs a hand down Alex's damp back, feeling him shiver.

In the nothing-light, his features are slack and hazy, and he tells Jack, "I should put some pants on at the very least, just in case."

Jack's going to grab for him, tell him *nah, no pants,* but he's not sure that's a thing he can do right now, the exact ways that fucking each other changes things between them, or if it changes anything at all.

"Don't wanna get caught with your pants down," Jack says and then cringes and groans. "Pretend I didn't say that."

Alex laughs, though, and Jack gives him a shove upright, feeling the uncomfortable sensation of dick slipping free. He ties off the condom and reaches over the sofa arm to stick it in the trash, zipping his jeans up and leaning forward with his elbows on his knees to stretch his back out.

Something changes, then, and Alex looks down at him, naked and silvery, so, *so* shamelessly wanting and almost visibly shocked by it. He touches Jack's face—and fuck, the only description that comes to mind is *reverently*—and tips him upward at the chin.

When he eventually mutters, "Come to bed," Jack has the subtle suspicion that's not what he'd planned to say.

"No pants?"

Alex snorts, all the delicate grace of the moment gone. "I'm gonna take them, 'cause you never know."

"Because maybe we'll have to run for our lives?"

Alex flicks the side of his face. "You do watch too many movies."

Chapter Eleven

This time when he opens his eyes, it's daylight.

Strange bed, foreign view out the window, warm body behind him; Jack's memories come like a hot flood, the smell of sex quickly after. He stretches and rolls over carefully onto his back, making sure none of Alex's body parts are disturbed, wants to look at him a little while exactly as he is.

He's sprawled out on his front, head turned away. The sheets are rolled low around his hips, resting in the curve of his spine. Jack pressed his tongue there at some point in the night, dreamlike as it was.

The night.

The whole damn night, recalled in a blur. Jack's woken up in bed with a government killer, shots fired and a smoking car wreck in the rearview; the cold light of day sure as hell takes the sleepy ease out of things.

"Do you have to think so loud?" Alex grumbles, and Jack's so startled he scoots away half a foot. Alex whips his head around, giving Jack a deadpan look.

He scrubs a hand across his stubble, staring at the ceiling.

"Sorry, I was just remembering why I'm actually here."

Alex is quiet a while, simply watching. Eventually he shifts up onto his elbows, back cracking when he rolls it—Jack really wishes he wouldn't do that, the lithe, obscene ripple of his naked spine.

This is the part where any normal person would be asking if Jack had any regrets. Alex asks, "Want coffee?" because what they're doing is anything but normal, and of course, Alex is accommodating like that, the things he's gonna be asking of Jack from now on.

"Yeah, coffee'd be great."

Alex briefly touches him on the arm before he pushes out of bed, grabbing a T-shirt and his boxers and somehow walking and dressing himself at the same time.

Jack aches in places way under-exercised, feels like he's pulled a shoulder out of joint, but deeper than that is the ache of satisfaction. It's a tricky thing, an unreliable emotion. Waking up with Richard in his bed used to satisfy him until the press hunt and Jack's father waving photographs in his face while Senator Leigh watched the study fire crackle, his back resolutely turned.

There's even more at stake here, conditions so imposing and vital they're paralyzing.

And then, Alex pads back into the bedroom, a steaming mug in each hand, and Jack's brain has the gall to immediately dismiss that entire thought process.

Alex waits for him to prop himself up in the pillows before

handing him the mug, sitting himself cross-legged in the middle of the mattress, bedhead and sleepy pallor making him look harmless.

"I can still hear your gears grinding," Alex tells him dryly round the lip of his mug.

It's good coffee, and Jack holds a sip on his tongue to buy himself a moment. "I am—possibly finally absorbing everything."

"I get that; it's a lot."

"And I'm still naked, which, y'know."

Alex smirks, eyes entirely fond. He starts to shift. "If you need some space, just say—"

"No." Jack's hand is wrapped around Alex's ankle whip-quick. He gives Alex a sheepish shrug. "I mean. No?"

"Wanna just pretend we're some other two dudes and make out all day?" Alex asks, but it's just a quip designed to make Jack laugh.

Last night Jack held Alex against the mattress, hands clasped and slow moving, and told him over and over how fucking beautiful he was. He can hear his own breathless voice in the dark even now, mortifyingly tender, promising the whole world.

He looks, *really* looks, at Alex in the clear morning light. He's carefully non-intrusive, young-looking and casually hunched, hands wrapped loosely around his cup. Jack had thought maybe fucking it out of his system might lessen the urgency of his attraction, take some of that painful edge off, but he was wrong.

He wants and he wants, and there's no relief from it.

This Alex, tired and coffee-smelling, is a minefield. The version that staged a fire and disobeyed orders to bring Jack here, too. The Alex that came to him in the park that night and the one that told him he *must be crazy too.*

"As tempting as that is," Jack huffs. "What, uh, what happens now?"

"Now I go back to my chief of staff and argue your case," Alex explains. His manner is easy, calming, no big deal. "If all goes well, you'll be under my protection; I'll be responsible for you."

"Wow, that's kinda hot."

Alex smirks, going on, "And then we wait for their direction."

"So you don't actually know what happens now?"

"I can guess."

"*I* can guess," Jack stresses. "I have to prove my dad's in cahoots with a bunch of organized criminals. I mean, that's great and all, but there are a few major flaws in this plan, like how do I get not killed the second I turn up on his doorstep, and how do I prove something the authorities couldn't for years?"

"Jack," Alex says. "Breathe, to start with."

"*Alex!*"

His hand curls warm and heavy over Jack's thigh under the covers. "Nobody is gonna throw you in the deep end here, okay? I won't let them."

You haven't, Jack thinks intensely. Doesn't say it, though, because Alex goes on.

"The government does not want your father in the Senate. Another hit on him will be a Hail Mary, but an *arrest*—that could mean the exposure of years of high-level corruption, weeding out assholes by the dozens, the hundreds. Think of the retrials, think of the disbarrings—"

"I wanna help, okay, but that's a lot to lay at one guy's feet," Jack interrupts shakily. Alex had that gleam in his eye again, an almost holy conviction.

Now, he frowns. "You're not just some guy, Jack."

"I'm not a fucking spook either."

Alex places his cup on one of the nightstands, leaning down to find his phone somewhere on the floor. He flips through it for a second, spinning it and showing Jack the picture of Jacob Kalhoff in his father's hallway.

"You might wanna quit acting like one, then."

Jack knocks the phone out of his hand, glaring right back at Alex's equally unimpressed glare. "Yesterday you reamed me for that picture," he points out.

"That was—" Alex looks away, out the window. "I was pissed, give me a break."

"It was personal, you mean."

Very quietly, Alex tells him, "Yeah," and then, dryly, "That right there is why professional boundaries were invented."

"Do you want professional boundaries?" Jack asks, a sinking

feeling in his chest. It's lucidity, he realizes. The very hard knowledge that a boundary might be both necessary and also impossible.

"Do you?"

"Dude," he whines, "I asked you first."

"What I want doesn't matter."

"*What*, like hell it doesn't!"

"Hey." The hand is back on his thigh. "Jack, listen to me, I'm not the one going on the line here. You and, and what *you* need right now is absolutely paramount, whatever it takes to make this easier. If you need a line, there'll be a line. Agents have sex with their assets all the time. It's—it's not a big deal. It doesn't have to be."

It's the exact opposite of Jack's impulses, to be reserved, to be careful.

His mouth is dry when he asks, "Would you sleep with me just because I needed it?"

Alex swallows, looking down at the rumpled sheets. "No."

"Why not? If agents sleep with assets all the time, if it's not a big deal, why not?" It's overwrought; he's not demanding sex, he wouldn't, but he needs to know—

"Because I have feelings for you," Alex says plainly. "It'd always be partly selfish." He pulls a wry face and adds, "Personal. I can only separate that out if you ask me to."

It means more to him than it should, hearing it like that. It's not like he didn't suspect, but motives are insidious things, and sexual attraction doesn't mean a damn thing in the face of them.

"I need you," he tells Alex hoarsely. "But, uh."

"I get it; it's okay."

Is it? Jack doesn't have a clue what he needs, truth be told, but Alex has shown this uncanny pattern of anticipating him. He knows he doesn't want to be accommodated, though, not at the exploitation of Alex's dutifulness. He doesn't want to be constantly questioning himself over either of their motives, over who's using who and how it might hurt when the fog's cleared.

Maybe it is for the best that they draw a line somewhere, just for now.

"Okay."

"Okay," Alex repeats, disconcertingly blank, studying the sheets again. "Okay," he says again, more decisively, and the word is losing all meaning. "I'm gonna have to leave you for a couple hours to straighten things out, but I'll be back."

Leave. He gets momentarily lightheaded, quipping, "You going down the fire escape?" to cover his ass.

"It's the only way I travel," Alex smirks, almost disarming Jack's defenses all over again.

Alex gets up, still blissfully half-naked. He opens up the bedroom closet and pulls out a T-shirt, idly telling Jack, "There's spare stuff in here, some of mine and my buddy's about—well, his shirts will fit you."

Jack looks down at his coffee, focusing hard, wets his dry lips and asks, "You're confident this is gonna work, right?"

"Absolutely."

"Sound less convinced," Jack deadpans. "Please."

Alex stands at the side of the bed, head cocked. "You gonna be okay here?" he asks softly.

"Yeah." Jack smiles. "Anyone comes in, I'll beat their asses like I did yours."

Alex scoffs. "You better hope they think you're hot, then, 'cause that's the only reason you got the drop on me."

He turns and leaves at that, with Jack staring after him, trying to think up something clever to say. He hears the bathroom door shut and the shower start, and Jack sits the whole while sipping his coffee, remembering, vividly, the night in his father's study.

Alex failed that night over Jack. He wonders what happens if Alex's superiors veto him and demand their prisoner.

It's a nerve-wracking train of thought; this moment of calm doesn't feel like a respite at all, more like a tightrope or a fuse, some amalgamation of both. Burning up the only bit of support under him, could give way at any second and send him tumbling down.

He thinks about his dad wondering where Jack's gone, if his paranoia is terrible enough to take this as the final betrayal it is. What would his mom say if she could see him right now—

"Jack?"

He looks up at the doorway, at Alex, dressed and leaning against the frame.

"Go," Jack tells him. "I'll be fine."

Alex nods slowly. "Just, uh, make yourself at home, okay?" He turns and disappears down the hall. Jack hears the front door close and lock—not taking the fire escape after all—and then he's alone.

He gets up, finally, swinging his legs over the side of the bed and navigating himself upright. The stiffness in his spine eases out, and he remembers how to relax, to breathe, now that Alex isn't here to suck all the air out of him.

Jack heads to the shower, figuring out the old taps, and finds Alex has left him a towel draped over the shower screen. It punches through him like a fist, hits him where he's already tender, but he stuffs it down to something manageable, wraps himself in it and finds a plain white T-shirt in the closet that's just a little too big for him.

In the kitchen he finds bread and butter, more coffee in the pot. He eats a slice of toast before his stomach rejects any further attempt at food, and the coffee sits badly too, making him slosh when he moves. He paces a few grooves in the carpets and floorboards, picks books off the shelves and flips through them.

Alex's large-shouldered friend is a fan of buildings, Jack learns in his pursuit of blissful distraction. There are sketches stuffed into architectural magazines, creative and a little bit weird, and cramped notes in book margins that look like the work of a stressed-out college hand.

There's a photo in a frame of a bunch of people—a family maybe, various likenesses in their faces—somewhere outdoorsy and soaked in sun. Behind it a photo of a tall, red-headed girl with a baby in her arms. Jack recognizes the locale of that one: Saint Matthew's church, looks like a christening.

An hour passes before he feels like he can sit down without jumping right back up again.

He settles on the sofa for a while, flicking all the way through the channels three times before braving the local news. It's not like he expects to see anything on there about what went down yesterday, but paranoia riles him up suitably anyway.

Except he's justified. His father appears, standing framed by the smoking remains of the backyard bushes, so it's probably a recording from yesterday. And Jack stares blankly at his mouth moving for whole seconds before he starts to hear the words.

"Both me and my son are fine, no one was hurt, thank God—"

The words *accidental garden fire at Congressman George Preston's residence, no casualties* scroll across the bottom of the screen.

"And will this incident put the brakes on your campaign, Congressman?" a woman with a microphone asks in a syrupy voice.

"Not at all, Suzanne," his father laughs. "For the people of

Broneburg and for my son, who despite the stress caused by this accident is always quick to remind his dad what's most important."

"You son of a bitch," Jack mutters. The picture changes to a flyby of a highway, some car chase out of town, and Jack mutes the drone of car engines and whir of sirens, the voiceover telling him the assailant's reached ninety-four and counting.

He doesn't know what he expected. Maybe not to be confronted with it so ham-handedly, but still—his dad acting like Jack's just upstairs minding his own business is almost hysterical. Will he have to endure this puppet show for the whole campaign? His father making various excuses for why his son can't come out to play. They have an interview with the Review in a few days; Jack's going to have to come down with a bad case of strep or something.

He could be dead, and there's no sobbing press conferences, no state-wide search. George is worried, all right—not about Jack's wellbeing, but about keeping things smooth.

Yeah, he doesn't know what he was expecting, but somehow he still has the capacity for surprise.

In the silence of the muted TV, the door lock rattles. Jack feels his heart kick up, a feeble rebellion against his resolve because he's only human after all, and he gets up like he's standing to attention, only feeling dumb about it when Alex is almost to the lounge.

Jack turns sheepishly, but it's not Alex in the doorway.

"Who—"

He must look visibly panicked, because the guy holds out both his hands, quickly stressing, "Hey, no, no, it's okay, I'm a friend, I'm Marlowe."

He's huge, tall and round with baby features. "Marlowe?"

"Wait," *Marlowe* says slowly; his voice is light and expressive. "Alex didn't tell you my name, did he?" Jack shakes his head, but his shoulders slump a notch. "Okay, let's start again, I'm Marlowe, I'm Alex's friend, and this is my apartment."

He holds out a hand to shake, and Jack steps forward to grasp it. "I guess you know who I am?"

"Nice to meet you, Jack." Marlowe grins. "That coffee I smell?" Jack nods again, following him into the kitchen to watch him heat the pot back up. "Alex messaged me to come check on you."

"Why, what's wrong?" Jack asks quickly.

"I don't know that anything is." Marlowe presses his back to the kitchen counter. "He just said he might be a little longer than anticipated."

Jack exhales shakily. "Wonderful."

Marlowe finds a mug, pours his coffee, and studies Jack curiously. He has kind and intelligent features, an easy manner. "I have no idea what's going on, obviously," he says and then corrects himself, "Okay, I'm not an idiot, I got some ideas." Jack huffs a laugh. "But uh, s'pretty heavy, right?"

"Yeah."

"Whoa, that heavy?"

"What's my face doing right now?" Jack asks dryly.

"Trying to cover inner turmoil."

"Oh, you're good."

Marlowe gestures him into the lounge, taking a seat on one of the sofas. Jack takes the other, TV still muted.

"It's a nice place," Jack says. "Thanks for letting me stay."

"Hey, don't mention it." Marlowe waves him away. "I don't even live here. We keep it going for nostalgia mostly."

"We?"

"Me and Aphra," he explains. Jack raises an eyebrow, and Marlowe smirks, explaining, "She's my sister. Our ma was in theatre, named us after playwrights."

"Explains the location."

"Aphra's worked at the playhouse since she was a kid, and I just loved the building. We bought this place years ago when it was derelict and worth pennies; now we rent it out cheap to the local struggling actor population."

"Hey, I might be out of a place soon. Wanna rent it to me?" Jack asks with a grin.

"I haven't gauged how much trouble you are yet," Marlowe quips.

Jack laughs. "Only rarely do I need to lay low for my life. This is highly out of character."

"I'd ask Alex to vouch for you, but the guy's crazy, so."

He laughs again, oddly thrilled to hear Alex's name in the context of someone else's experiences. Someone infinitely more qualified to talk about him than Jack. "How long have you known him?"

"Since high school, lotta years." Marlowe narrows his eyes, sly if Jack ever saw it. "How about yourself?"

"Not long," he hedges.

"How bad do you wanna ask me what he was like?"

Jack grits his teeth, hands clenched and hanging between his knees. "Not at all. You gonna tell me?"

Marlowe chuckles. "You ever have one of those bastards you grew up with that was just good at everything? That was Alex."

"The kid that everybody hates?"

"Yeah, but Alex was impossible to hate," Marlowe muses. "It was a hard life." Jack bites down on a smile; that, he can relate to. "Am I allowed to ask how you met him?"

"It's—complicated."

"Damn, thought as much."

"We're not..." Jack trails off, kind of hoping that will be enough.

"Hey, for all I know, you're the prince of Geneva and he's your bodyguard."

Jack huffs. "What does that make you?"

"His temporary stand-in. Sorry, bud, but you're probably gonna die."

Jack's about to pry some more, but the newsreel from the townhouse plays again in his peripheral vision, and he stares at the silent movement of his dad's mouth, hearing the words in his head.

"Every time that asshole's face appears on my television I have fantasies about going blind," Marlowe says, and Jack's attention snaps back to him. "Oh, you're not a supporter, are you?"

"No," Jack breathes, barely audible. "No, no way."

The camera pans over the charcoaled garden, same words as before scrolling past on the news ticker.

"Shame his whole house didn't burn down with him inside."

Jack tries to laugh. "Yeah." He swallows down the spit in his mouth.

"He's almost put me out of business. Who's even voting for him?"

"Maybe no one has to," Jack mutters.

"Or everyone thinks he's something he's not."

"What d'you mean?"

"Ex-military, salt-of-the-earth family man? Tall, handsome, and charismatic? He's practically tailor-made for this shit."

"And, uh, you don't think he's any of those things?"

"I think he's a lotta things, I think he's the reason Alex—" Marlowe's voice raises and cracks. He stutters and stalls for a second, looking at Jack sheepishly. "Never mind, ignore me running my mouth like an idiot. You ever have that one trigger?

Preston's face is apparently mine."

Jack burns with wanting to hear the end of that sentence. He's staring, he knows he is, but he can't seem to quit.

Marlowe shakes his head. "Anyway." He pulls out his cell. "I should let him know you're doing okay."

"Tell him on behalf of the country of Geneva to get his ass back here," Jack jokes softly, watching the way it calms Marlowe down after his little slip. He flashes Jack a grin and taps something into his phone, waiting a little while before putting it away. Jack supposes Alex isn't immediately available right now.

His anxiety climbs up a notch.

"Hey, don't worry about it," Marlowe comforts. "If you are in fact worried, that is." Jack cocks a shoulder, a sort of shrug; noncommittal. "He once disappeared for eight weeks with no warning, no explanation, no nothing. He came back just fine. Well, fine-ish. Alive, at any rate."

"*Eight weeks*?"

"Yup. I still, to this day, don't know where he went."

Probably across some war-torn border somewhere, eight weeks of radio silence. Or melting into another person's life to get close to a target, collecting intelligence or something much worse.

"I'd go outta my mind if that was someone I cared about," Jack considers quietly.

"Hard to hate, even more difficult to love."

He can't think on that right now, asking instead, "How'd he

even get into all this?" even though he knows it's not Marlowe's place to say.

"Circumstance," Marlowe tells him vaguely. "Just like all of us."

Jack thinks about Shawn and Sol. They've got to be wondering where he is right now, too, and it might be only a matter of time before Sol storms on up to the townhouse looking for him, especially with the news story circulating so rabidly.

He'd borrow Marlowe's phone and call her, if he wasn't almost positive his dad would find out somehow.

Speaking of—Jack hears the hum of Marlowe getting a message before Marlowe does.

He points it out, and Marlowe checks it.

"He's on his way."

Jack's whole fucking body reacts to this news; his chest goes tight, arms and legs weak. It's some awful concoction of fear and relief, both draining and energizing.

Marlowe heads to the kitchen to make more coffee, apparently at explicit request from Alex, and Jack sits with the muted TV, idly watching the weather guy gesture out a lengthy warm front that Jack wouldn't put money on ever reaching the city.

The keys jangle in the lock at the same time as Marlowe passes Jack a mug, and they both look toward the door, Alex sort of halting there looking awkwardly between them. It's a three-way standoff, and Jack feels like he hasn't seen Alex in days instead of hours, captivated by the sight of him with his cheeks flushed from the wind and his hair mussed up.

"Uh, coffee, Alex?" Marlowe asks and then disappears into the kitchen with all the subtlety of a brick through the window.

Jack stands and Alex steps forward, and they meet halfway, Jack aching to touch but pulling it back before he gives into the urge. He looks instead, for signs of stress, for injuries even, and then just to look, because Alex hasn't stopped being fucking beautiful just because Jack's too messed up to deal with it.

"Are you okay?" he asks on a breath and Alex cocks his head, smiling wryly.

"I'm fine." Jack raises his eyebrows, and Alex relents, "I got reamed, but I'm *fine*."

"Reamed," Jack repeats flatly.

"And then grudgingly patted on the back."

"What does that mean?"

"Means," Alex starts, checking over Jack's shoulder. His gaze locks somewhere back there, his expression quickly darkening, and he lowers his voice. "Means your life is about to get very difficult."

"That's me done here then, boys," Marlowe says loudly, and Jack turns, watches Marlowe put Alex's cup on the coffee table and sees his father's bleating face back on the TV screen right where Alex is staring. "Coffee for two and enjoy your day."

He grabs Alex's hand, pulling him into a one-armed hug and

saying something close to his ear that Jack steps away for in an effort not to overhear. When he's done, Jack gives him a smile, telling him, "Thanks for all this, Marlowe."

"Hope to see you again, Jack, once all this"—he gestures with his hand, a whirling motion—"whatever is done with."

And on that he leaves, with Alex visibly cringing and Jack trying not to notice. He sits down instead, picking up his mug and taking a long drink, waiting for Alex to sit and do the same.

"Lay it on me, then."

Alex presses his lips together. "Don't you wanna make small talk first?"

"My life is about to get very difficult," Jack repeats.

Alex takes a long breath, and Jack watches his Adam's apple bob. The silence seems to stretch out forever, and Jack kind of wants it to, kind of doesn't. "How are you at lying to your father?"

"Pretty good. I've had a lot of practice."

"Can you deceive him into believing that the person who tried to kill him was a known associate of his?" Alex asks, and Jack blinks; he really was not expecting that. "Specifically Jacob Kalhoff."

"Why—" Jack stutters. Lotta whys he can think up right now. "Why Kalhoff?"

"His acquittal didn't protect him from a civil suit and a very tenacious family has a mind to drag his ass back to court. After he went to see your father last week, it seems he flew straight out to

Guatemala. That scream trust issues to you?"

"You think my dad intends to let him hang this time?"

"I think your father's clever enough to know Kalhoff probably thinks that."

"So, let me get this straight," Jack clarifies. "You want me to convince my dad that his long-term business buddy put a hit out on him?"

"Yes."

"To make him believe I'm loyal to him, so he'll trust me enough to expose his dirtiest, best-kept secret."

"Something like that."

"After disappearing off the map for twenty-four hours from the scene of an accident where one of his private security got shot."

"Yeah, that about sums it up."

Jack stares, mouth hanging open. "And—and not die or get locked back up inside the house while I'm at it."

Alex moves quickly from the sofa to the edge of the coffee table, his knees almost touching against Jack's. He leans forward, expression grim, and slowly presses a palm upward against the underside of one of Jack's hands, stroking with his fingertips.

"You don't have to do this."

"Yeah, Alex, I think we covered that one already. I do have to do this."

"You could run," Alex says, eyes wide. He's fucking serious.

Jack curls his hand, wrapping his fingers loosely around

Alex's wrist. "Would you run?"

"That's different."

"What did he do to you?" Jack asks softly. "Why do you hate him like you do? You stood in that study and apologized to me for killing him, but you were gonna do it anyway."

"It's my *job*—"

"Must be exhausting to hate everyone you end on the job that much."

"Is what he is not enough of a reason?" Alex's pulse is quick against Jack's fingers. "Look, we don't have time for this."

He's right; Jack's pushing again, crossing the self-imposed line already.

"Alex," Jack starts, hardly more than a breath, "you know I'm not gonna run from this. You knew that when you left earlier, you knew that last night when we fucked, you knew that yesterday when you got me out of the house."

Alex looks down, close enough that Jack can see the light from outside follow the curve of his eyelashes. He doesn't speak, but Jack knows it means *yes* all the same.

"So. How do we do this?" Jack asks decisively, feeling everything but. Alex squeezes his hand, trailing his fingertips back over Jack's palm as he lets go.

"We act very fast," he tells Jack. He pulls a phone out of his pocket, an ancient-looking thing with a green-gray screen and rubber buttons, and hands it over. "Things are about to get tricky."

Chapter Twelve

"Hey, Sol?"

"Jack, where the *hell* have you been?"

"I'm fine, let me explain."

"I've been going outta my mind!"

"Some shit went down at the house, but I'm okay, I'm good."

"Your phone's been off, your dad was on the news—"

"I know. I don't wanna explain over the phone, but I have to speak to my father first."

"Where are you?"

"I'll explain everything later, okay? Just give me a few days."

"I don't like this, Jack."

"Me neither, Sol. Me neither."

Chapter Thirteen

He takes a long inhale of breath.

The air is cool outside this afternoon, like all the heat got sucked away with last night's storm. The wind whips his hair, and the clouds still brood in thick layers of gray and Jack moves with a sort of steely purpose, one foot in front of the other until he can see the townhouse up ahead.

Five minutes ago he'd felt Alex's stare bore against the side of his face like a drill bit, sharp and urgent.

"Don't say it," Jack warned him. "I'm doing it. Shut up."

"It'd help if you got out of the car," Alex had said lightly, teasing, and Jack had rolled his eyes. "You know what to do if things go balls up."

"What a great turn of phrase."

"Jack."

"I know what to do, *God*."

He'd held the car door in a loose fist, and Alex had told him, "I'm not gonna let anything bad happen to you," and, "You need to trust me to look out for you, 'cause that's what I'm gonna be doing," and Jack had believed him, really, but logic has less sway compared to the dread of being back here.

He takes another long, long inhale.

Charlie's face drops in shock the second he recognizes Jack approaching. He's sitting on the same outside bench they'd eaten lunch on so many afternoons, Joel with his back turned, gesturing about something, but he spins when Charlie stands up.

"Jesus, feels like I'm lookin' at a ghost," he says, and Jack throws his arms out sheepishly as a greeting. "Your dad ain't here, though, and we're under pretty strict orders to—"

The screech of tires startles all of them, and Jack turns his head over his shoulder—*it's fine, it's just the van, you expected this*—and sees two people he doesn't recognize clamber out of the surveillance van.

They approach him, a woman with a radio in her hand and a guy who looks straight-up bored. What they're doing is blocking him in, keeping him there; as if him coming back here was just to play ding dong ditch.

He turns back to Charlie and Joel. "Am I going to him or is he coming to me?"

They both look pretty nonplussed, but the tinny voice on the radio behind him tells him the former. He's surprised when Charlie steps forward, hand up to signal a halt.

"Let me take him."

The woman considers it, shrugging and speaking into her radio. "Marquez is bringing him now."

"I gotta grab some stuff first," he tells Charlie, and Charlie nods, leading him into the townhouse, where Jack can still smell the charcoal remnants of yesterday's fire.

They climb the stairs in silence, get to Jack's bedroom door in silence, but once they're inside, Charlie leans against the frame and quips, "That was some escape, kiddo."

Jack starts throwing clothes into a travel bag. "It wasn't an escape."

"Two guys are in the hospital."

"I swear I had nothing to do with it." He cocks his head over his shoulder. "You think I'd come back here like a dumbass if I'd gone to all that trouble to get myself out?"

"I just assumed you weren't that bright." Charlie smirks, and Jack scoffs and heads to the bathroom to grab his toothbrush. Charlie calls after him, "I'm sorry, by the way."

"For what?" He walks back into the hall, confronted by Charlie's uncomfortably scrunched-up face. "You look constipated, man."

"For, y'know."

Jack raises an eyebrow. "Imprisoning me?"

"Yeah, that."

"Hey, what could you do?" He shrugs, hauling the bag over one shoulder. "A job's a job."

"Yeah," Charlie grumbles. "But it felt shitty, so I had to tell you, y'know." Jack nods. "You ready to go?"

"Let's do this."

The car's already there when they head back outside, and Jack's having momentary flashbacks for a wild second, yesterday's utter chaos versus today's more methodical dread. It's difficult to reconcile the fact that the fire, the crash, all went down just over twenty-four hours ago.

Charlie herds him into the backseat, and they're off.

"How are Wade and the driver?" Jack asks, realizing he probably should've checked up on that before.

"Shot and concussed," Charlie tells him nonchalantly. "They're gonna be fine, though."

"Good."

"I'd ask what happened, but I'm sure you wanna tell your old man first."

"Yeah." Jack shifts in his seat. "Why'd you wanna bring me personally, anyway? There some kinda reward or something?"

Charlie snorts. "I wish. No, I seriously thought you were dead meat yesterday, and everything before..." He trails off. "I wanted to make sure you were doing okay."

"I'll live," Jack says. "He's at the summer house in Cedar Heights, isn't he?"

"Bingo."

"It's not exactly a top secret location."

"It's gated, plus there's plenty of space to hit a moving target if we have to." Charlie keeps flicking him little looks. "I think he's been expecting you, y'know."

Jack reacts carefully. "Really?"

"Yeah, earlier he told Joel and me to watch out for anything *strange*." He does air quotes. "I mean that's generally what we do already, right? But then you show up."

"Well, unless he's psychic, I don't see how he could."

Charlie shrugs, and Jack doesn't push it. Evidence, though, that his dad was listening in on Sol's phone line after all.

Cedar Heights takes them over the high roads, way above the Wilbec, and back down again into the valley where the river widens out and slows to mild waves lapping at the bank.

"I haven't been here in, God, must be fifteen years or more," Jack tells Charlie. "Far as I know, neither has my dad."

They pass through the community gates, the driver showing the gate security some ID, and Charlie whistles as they drive down the wooded road and pull into the long driveway of the summer house.

It's like Jack remembers it: white wood exterior and almost wall-to-wall windows, the porch that wraps around the whole front and left side of the building.

"How'd you know he'd be here?" Charlie asks as they pull up.

"Just a guess." Jack climbs out of the car, leading Charlie up the path. "The other summer place is in Florida, and I knew he wouldn't leave the state. Plus he hates hotels."

More security lines the long porch, waiting for them, and

Jack's dread turns his stomach. He feels faintly nauseous with it, getting thoroughly frisked at the door by a rough-looking guy in a black backwards cap not helping any.

The smell of dust and disuse is strong inside, and there are cleaners everywhere, dusting and polishing, trying to make the place livable. Jack was right—it looks like his dad hasn't been here in years either.

Charlie cocks his head close and tells Jack, "He's set up in the dining room."

"This where you leave me?"

"Sorry, kiddo, I got a door to get back to."

"Thanks, Charlie," Jack says awkwardly. "For, y'know."

Charlie slaps him on the shoulder. "Sure thing, man."

Jack doesn't watch him leave, busy steeling his nerve. This place is a graveyard to him, nothing but memoirs of the dead in the creaky floorboards and shelves lined with photo frames and dust. His father couldn't have forced this issue to a more awful location if they'd done it over his mom's tombstone.

He makes a show of getting stuck behind a man dragging a vacuum cleaner for a few crucial extra seconds to collect his sanity, and then he's at the dining room door, raising a hand to knock.

It's Boyce who answers; joy of joys.

He gives Jack a cold smirk and holds the door open for him, and Jack makes eye contact with his father standing at the head of the oval table, cold and lacking any sort of patience.

"The prodigal son returns," George drawls.

"According to the news, he never left."

His father loses just a fraction of his composure, but he recovers quickly, mouth a sneering line. "Care to explain to me why I have two men in the hospital while you're walking about just fine?"

"You might wanna kick Boyce out for this conversation."

His father narrows his eyes. "I don't think so."

"What d'you think I'm gonna do, Dad?" Jack snaps. "Your guys already frisked me. I can't exactly glare you to death, can I?"

"I said no."

"I'm your *son*," Jack shouts. "Haven't you punished me enough already?"

"Where have been, Jack?" his father asks darkly, and Jack's absolutely going about this all wrong, being too *Jack* too quickly.

Alex told him to be methodical, keep his calm; appeal to his father like a businessman, not like a son.

"I know who sent him."

His father's expression darkens. He leans both hands against the dining table and, after a stretch of silence, he orders, "Boyce, wait outside," and they're swiftly left alone. "Explain yourself."

Jack steps around the table and tells him urgently, "I want your word that I can walk out of here. I'm not your prisoner or your property, and if you try lock me up again, you're not getting shit out of me."

His father raises his eyebrows. "That sounds like negotiating."

"Call it whatever you want, but you have no idea what kinda danger you're in right now."

He's not easy to frighten, George Preston, but Jack's about the closest thing to an emotional anchor his dad has, and it seems to resonate on some level, a tiny, uncontrollable twitch of concern around his father's mouth.

"You're a free man, Jack. There's nothing stopping you from doing whatever you please."

Jack doesn't scoff at that blatant bit of bullshit. "What did you do to piss off Jacob Kalhoff, Dad?"

Oh, that's wonderful; his father's face drops, his steely eyes go wide. "No. No, he's—"

"Out of the country, yeah, I know. Guatemala sure is nice this time of year." He thinks that sells it—*thank you*, Alex—and Jack pulls out from his pocket a tiny ball of white powder wrapped in clingy plastic and throws it down on the table. "What d'you suppose this is?"

His father picks it up between his finger and thumb, studying it closely. "Rohypnol?"

"Kalhoff's people offered me two million to get you to drink it, take you somewhere secluded, and wait for collection."

George smiles ruefully, shaking his head. "His people." That doesn't mean anything to Jack, and his stomach tosses uneasily. "And did his *people* say what he wanted with me?"

"You have something that could ruin him, and you're the kind of two-faced snake that would."

"Oh, so it's an interrogation they're after."

"I don't think you're supposed to survive it," Jack says flatly.

His father visibly grits his teeth. His breath comes a little shaky. Jack's too off-kilter to be bolstered by it, too fundamentally aware like someone dealing with a tamed but wild animal, but it's a step in the right direction, the kind of reaction he's hoping to see.

"Why would anyone think you'd do this?" his father asks roughly.

"Because he's just like you, isn't he? Thinks he can make people jump on his dime."

"No, it doesn't make sense."

"This is what happens when you get into bed with *real* criminals," Jack blurts, panicked. "You asked for this, Dad. It was only a matter of time."

"Did they threaten you?"

"Of course they fucking threatened me! What d'you think we were doing for a whole twenty-four hours, playing checkers?"

That seems to sit better, but Jack still needs to wrangle his slippery emotions under control.

"So you said you'd do it."

"I said what I had to," he says flatly. "Getting real tired of being pushed around, though." That, at least, isn't a lie.

"Do these people trust you?"

Saying *yes* would be naïve, so Jack goes with, "I don't know."

"Then perhaps someone's bluffing," his father drawls and doesn't elaborate.

Jack compulsively swallows, *fuck*. "Well, I wouldn't wanna call it. A rock and a hard place is a pretty unfortunate position to be." His father hums. "You think you're untouchable, don't you? You're not. You're *not*, and they proved it, and you cannot face it!"

"You don't know what I've survived." His dad sneers. "And all without a lick of help from you."

It brings Jack to a stone-cold stop, physically flinching backwards. "What—"

"So don't be too surprised when I say *get out of my sight* so I can deal with this mess myself."

A freezing shiver works its way up Jack's spine and out through his limbs. His throat feels like it's flexing, words hard to squeeze out. "Do you know what they'll do to me?" he asks, and it's a genuine fear; *you could run*—but could he ever run fast enough? "Do you even care?"

"Don't get"—his father actually stutters there—"fucking emotional on me."

"I saved you," Jack spits. "And I risked my ass for your worthless life *again* by coming back here to try to reason with you when I could've run and left you to fucking die." He fists his trembling hand around the burner phone in his pocket and hopes for the time to call for help, sure, but if these were to be his last words, then he'd be glad. "I shoulda just let them kill you."

Jack backs up to the doorway.

His father grins.

"So why didn't you, eh?" he asks, savagely gleeful. "Come on, son, tell me what you really think!"

"Because you're my dad! You're my family!"

"And...?"

"And I think you better cough up a reasonable counteroffer or prepare to be looking over your shoulder for the rest of your existence." Jack halts a foot from the door. "I think I'm the only chance you've got."

There's a long silence. Jack calculates how quickly he could swing open the door, duck Boyce, and head for the back patio. He'd have more time out the back, more space to call Alex before someone got a hold of him. There's the river, if it came to that, and the woods beyond it.

"The only chance I've got," his father repeats softly. "That makes you very powerful indeed."

Jack guesses it does. It hits him low and unkind, that maybe part of the appeal is just this: lording it over his father for a while, making himself the single most vital thing in his father's world.

Making himself needed.

Trust his dad to hone in on that.

"Maybe I'm more like you than you think I am," Jack says quietly.

His father appraises him. "Maybe you are."

Jack collects his shattered pieces, taking a long breath. "So, what now?"

"Call your new friends and buy some time. I need to think."

"That mean you trust me?"

"I don't trust anybody, Jack," his father tells him simply. "Call them."

He thumbs, old-school-like, through the phone to the number Alex gave him and it rings once, twice, and then Alex picks up, his voice so achingly vivid that it cripples Jack for just a second.

He clears his throat. "Hey. It's me."

Alex's voice is very quiet on the line. "Just reply yes or no, okay?"

"Okay."

"We tracked your GPS to a place in Cedar Heights, is that where you are?"

"Yeah."

Down the line Jack can hear a steady click and whir like the sound of equipment. "Are you feeling safe?"

He swallows. "Yeah."

"Is he buying the story?"

"I need a few days; this place is too hot right now."

"*Jack*, are you safe?"

"It's fine, don't worry about it. I said I'd get it done, and I will."

His father's gaze is steady on the dining table, intently

concentrating, and Alex blows out a breath, audibly restraining himself. "You call me if you need me, Jack, and I will get you out."

"I know that."

So softly, Alex tells him, "Good luck," and Jack disconnects the call quickly before he can react under the weight of it.

His father is oddly blank-faced, and Jack waits in vain for him to speak.

"*Dad?*"

"Jack, shut up."

He balls his hands into fists, furiously biting his tongue. Waiting on his father's time is a familiar sensation, and it could be twenty years ago for how childlike it makes him feel. A far cry away from this moment, so thick with unease and hostility Jack could reach out and snap the air.

The problem is his father responded best to Jack's anger over his rationality, but he hates to be confronted or called out and he despises Jack's impulsiveness. It's a game of creating uncertainty, and Jack knows this is just how his dad likes to play.

"Stick around, Jack," he's told, belatedly. "Don't stray too far."

"What're you gonna do?"

"Figure it out like I always do," his father dismisses; Jack supposes it's a start. He's given his dad a tight scale of days. There aren't a lot of options at hand. "In the meantime, we carry on as normal. Suzanne will be here tomorrow night for the interview and tonight—tonight I'd like you to come somewhere with me."

Jack doesn't have to ask where; there's only one place his father disappears to once night falls. That—he *really* wasn't expecting that. "Why?"

"Call it a show of faith for your old man."

"You wanna parade me around in front of your lodge buddies?"

His father raises an eyebrow. "We still have a campaign to win, Jack."

Jack's never had an invite like this before. Social functions, benefits, rallies, yes, but his father's holy land?

The *we* sits uncomfortably, too.

"Fine," he agrees shortly.

He's dismissed with a hand-wave, a quipped, "Be ready at nine," and he doesn't need to be told twice, almost tripping over himself to get out of the room.

He makes his way urgently through the house, ignoring the people everywhere making this place feel like a museum. He's moving too intently, he thinks without being able to slow down; desperation written all over him as he strides through the hall, then the lounge, then out through the open patio doors. He's itching for his phone, too, to contact Alex, to fall right into that safety net.

He's no good at going to war with his own nature.

It's only outside that he feels the ground rebalance itself and the oppressive sense of foreboding lift. To overanalyze every detail of the conversation he just had would be an open door to madness. What's done is done; he can't take it back now.

Instead he looks out over the back of the property, letting memory grip him.

The grass stretches down beyond the stone patio slabs right to the river, another place Jack spent a lot of time as a kid, except the days here were isolated and tinged with worry.

They used to fight, he remembers. The townhouse floorboards made for good acoustics and his parents could put on quite a show. Then his mom would bundle Jack into the back of a cab and bring him here to get away, just the two of them. He'd rattle around this huge place looking for stuff to do, swim in the river when it was calm, throw rocks and sketch the ripples and currents when it wasn't.

Jack had spent the long days resenting his mom for dragging him away from the city.

He guesses, now, that distance from each other was the whole point of the summer house and the place down in Florida.

If she'd lived—well, he doesn't think she and his dad would've lasted long at all. Maybe George Preston was heading down this path regardless of his wife's death.

The wind whips up the hazelnut trees on the riverbank, makes the water run faster, and Jack sees her superimposed there, blonde hair blowing around her face, linen pants and the bright-colored shirts she always wore. She taught him to roast and shell the hazelnuts when they were ripe and they'd sit right here on the patio to eat them, the clay chimenea all fired up for warmth.

Jack blinks the blurriness out of his eyes.

He hates the moments he feels the closest to her; they leave a hollowness in his gut that takes time to fill back up. When she first passed away, people told him to keep her memory alive, remember the good times, but all he could cling to without falling apart was that last promise. The injustice and self-martyrdom was easier than the grief.

That's the thing he took from her in the end: a small slice of morphine-induced sentimentality for a man for whom she was only clinging to the good times.

She deserved better than Jack's bitterness, the laying of his issues at her gravestone. He turns and heads back inside wearily.

It's disconcerting to be left alone like this. He'd expected a guard following him around the house at the very least, and he can't shake the sensation of being watched despite that. He finds himself looking for cameras in the halls and bedrooms until he locates the one his bag has been dumped in, white-painted and nondescript like all of them are.

He pulls off his jacket and Marlowe's too-big shirt and swaps it out for one of his own. He considers texting Alex asking what to do with it, an opening of sorts, but it's an impulse for normal people in normal situations, and Jack doesn't entirely trust his own risk assessment at the moment, the off-kilter way he's feeling, the need for some kind of validation after the questionable way things went down with his father.

But God*damn* does he want to talk to Alex.

Because there's no way to dull the memory of his fingers knuckle-deep inside Alex or the tight heat of him stretched around Jack's cock. How quick and hard he'd come or how Alex had looked splayed out on the bedsheets afterwards, Jack crawling up between his legs to kiss him hard again.

Being rescued from a shitty situation does things to a guy, he figures. It's bound to. There's a billion-dollar market built off the back of that trope for a reason, and he's not enamored enough of his own masculinity to deny it turned his infatuation up to blinding. But the thing about infatuation is its brevity.

He's wanted Alex abstractly, the physical of him, since they fought on his dad's study floor. And then more than physically, Alex's wit and mystery like a baited fish-hook embedding under his ribs after the night in the city.

But Alex is not an unknown quantity anymore. Jack's had him, unwrapped the mystery, and Jack's either lost interest or he hasn't and, despite asking for a line to be drawn, he pretty obviously fucking *hasn't*. The only way forward is to fall the rest of the way and right now Jack feels a black hole at his feet, teetering on the event horizon of a whole new universe.

Whether his father is manipulated or not, Jack will very soon lose what's left of his family. He'll deal with the cataclysmal public fallout, maybe he'll slink away ruined as a traitor. Perhaps he'll get arrested or killed, who fucking knows?

It's a precarious edge; leaves little room for reckless love affairs. Afterwards, though—

He needs to lie down, conserve his energy for tonight, because while Alex has ceased to be an unknown quantity, everything else has apparently upended in the changeover, and he doesn't know when he's going to need it.

He grabs the phone and tells Alex *He's taking me to the lodge at 9, no clue why*, resolving to keep it professional.

A minute later he gets a reply: *There'll be a team nearby in case of emergency.*

He deletes all trace of the messages straight away, rolling over onto his side to stare out of the window and hope for sleep. *This is where things gets tricky*, Alex had said. But Alex said a lot of things in the past twenty-four hours, and Jack drifts to the sound of his voice, the gentle encouragement turning into helpless moans.

Chapter Fourteen

He fastens and unfastens the black tie around his neck more times than the number of hours he'd managed to sleep.

Showered and shaved, folded neatly into a crisp white shirt and tailored black dress pants delivered to his room by what he can only assume was a ghost, he looks at his reflection, at his carefully combed back hair and shiny shoes, and feels armored.

One too many James Bond movies, clearly, but the effect is overall bolstering. He looks pretty damn hot.

He hates ties, though. Hates them with a passion. They're constricting and uncomfortable and in this atmosphere of uncertainty could definitely be used against him as an easy murder weapon.

But his dad sent up a black tie, so Jack's going to wear the damn tie.

He slips on the suit jacket, buttons it, unbuttons it, buttons it again. Then he grabs his phone and updates Alex.

I'm wearing a suit, if you can believe that and then *We're setting off soon, don't let me die.*

There's a knock at the door as he deletes the messages.

"Come in."

The door creaks open, and his father appears out of the dark. "Downstairs in five."

Jack looks at him in the mirror. "You couldn't send up a messenger?"

"Wanted to check you'd dressed yourself appropriately."

Jack turns around, spreading his arms. "Highly."

He's studied closely; maybe his dad's looking for a collar out of place or the wrong amount of tucking in, evidence Jack's screwed up the Godforsaken tie. For once he seems appeased.

"Good enough. Come on."

George switches off the light, leaving Jack in the eagerly graying darkness and forcing him to follow.

He hasn't walked in dress shoes in a long time, and they lack traction on the hall carpets—no good for running if he has to. How the hell did Bond do it? They get to the downstairs hall, cleaning staff all gone now and the place looking and smelling infinitely fresher than it did earlier. There's only an ancient standing lamp switched on in the corner and the outside porch lights faintly pressing through the window blinds.

His father speaks to Boyce at the front door and then gestures to Jack, leading them outside.

It's mild, still windy with a clear sky. The car sits, dark and reflecting the stars, in the drive, and they climb into it—Jack, his father, and then Boyce.

They drive in silence a while. Jack notices they stick strictly to the main roads even though he's aware of a half-dozen quicker routes from the various As to Bs. His father's been avoiding the backstreets and secluded roads, obviously.

Jack's anxiety manages to tip the scale over his better senses, his father too silent and stoic a figure beside him. "So—why are you taking me to the place you used to use to get away from me?"

"A learning experience," is all his father has to say about that, gazing out of the window.

It does nothing to calm his nerves. "Learning how to drink whiskey for twelve hours and stay standing?"

His dad cracks a very brief smile at that, a reaction that doesn't even appear calculated. "Just play nice, Jack. Don't forget why we perform this play every two years."

"Yes, sir," Jack drawls.

The journey takes an age, sound of the engine humming the only thing keeping him sane. He doesn't see why they can't put on the radio or something, unless his dad wants him on edge; a distinct possibility.

By the time they brake, the rattling sound of loose gravel caught in the wheels, Jack's itching out of his suit. All his skin feels animated, yearning for movement, and he's trying defiantly not to fidget and give away his discomfort, anything to deprive his father of the satisfaction.

Both back doors are opened simultaneously by men in black

waistcoats. They climb out onto a semi-circle of driveway that pulls up close to a stone building. It sits in the middle of a stretch of flatland so huge the surrounding treelines are almost swallowed up by the dark. The lodge itself is a large, brick structure, entirely symmetrical, with steps leading up to the heavy front doors.

They're in the middle of nowhere, it seems. The road back and the lawns dotted with little solar lights go on forever.

"Jack."

He whips around to face his father.

"I didn't bring you here to stand outside all night."

Jack swallows and nods. Boyce takes them to the foot of the stairs but no farther, and Jack guesses he's not coming with them, doesn't know whether he's pleased or unnerved by that fact.

The two vested men pull open the front doors to let them into an echoing hall with black-and-white tiled floors and dark oak wall paneling. There's a lengthy desk with a coat check area set between two curving staircases that meet in the middle high above them.

Doors line the walls, some curtained, and the whole place smells richly of cinnamon and beeswax. The man behind the front desk *beams* at them in his red suede jacket, and Jack is reminded uncomfortably—not to mention unsubtly—of *The Shining*.

"Mr. Preston." He nods at Jack's father, and then at Jack. "And Mr. Preston. Any coats?"

"No, Tom, none tonight."

"The guest bar, then?"

"That's right."

They're politely herded into a corridor on the left side of the hall, and Jack leans close to his father, asking quietly out of the corner of his mouth, "The guest bar?"

"The only place non-members are allowed."

They come out the other side into a cozy bar, amber-lit and carpeted in royal blue, a dark-wood counter shining under spotlights all along one wall. There are booths and tables, but the place is reasonably full and many of the men are standing, clustered and talking in groups. Some of them are familiar faces at a glance—old memories and a million of them at that.

Jack's father hands him a scotch with ice from a man carrying a tray and, without any preamble, clinks his cufflink against the side of his own glass to get the attention of the room.

That's when Jack sees them: Richard Leigh and his father, the senator. Both of them standing around a tall round table near the back.

Richard is clearly not expecting Jack either, and they stare, wide-eyed, at each other across the quieting room. It's been years—*years*. He's wearing a suit much like Jack's but far more comfortably, and a wedding ring glittering on his left hand.

Jesus.

"As you know, I asked some of you to be here tonight," his father announces to his audience. "The others I didn't ask are

197

presumably here for the free bar I'm footing." A little ripple of indulgent laughter circles the room. "I had hoped to do this in the main suite, but since my son keeps dragging his heels on joining our prestigious brotherhood, the guest bar will have to do." This is going nowhere good, Jack quickly realizes with an awful swelling dread. "Most of you here have known us for a lot of years now, many since Jack was just a boy, and you all know I've been eagerly awaiting this day. So, without further rambling, I'm proud to announce—"

Oh, God.

"—Jack's engagement."

The men erupt into a round of applause, a few voices ring out in the din, and, incomprehensibly, all Jack can do is stare at Richard Leigh and the grim set of his face as he claps along too.

"Smile, Jack," his father tells him with a squeeze to the shoulder. "Play along like a good boy."

"This your way of putting me back in my place?" he asks, shaping his face into a smile and hoping it looks even remotely like one. "Putting yourself back on top?"

"Your power is an illusion, son." Another squeeze of his shoulder. "You're nothing if I say you're not and don't you forget it."

He can't forget, can he? Because everything is about dominance with his father, even apparent good will. He can't let himself be helped without exerting his control.

"You keep pushing me, and I will walk away and leave you to fend for yourself," Jack grits out.

"No you won't. You can't." His father gestures to a little throng of people, speaking around his own smile-for-show. "You're physically and emotionally incapable of ever really walking away from me, Jack, and the sooner you can admit that to yourself, the sooner we can move forward."

Jack's mouth goes dry. He's wrong—his father is wrong—

He's—

He's eight years old and grudgingly trying out for little league with his dad watching from the stands; he's fourteen and bringing home a girl who's pretty and smells like lavender for his father's scrutiny; he's eighteen and living in the barracks at Pall Hill and hating every second; he's twenty-one and leaving art school over spring break to join his father's campaign.

Jack's twenty-nine and fighting an assassin in the dark, involving himself left and right in a shady conspiracy, walking right back up to the doors of his father's fortress like a lamb to the slaughter.

He's waiting, even now, for a single *thank you*.

"Who is she, then, Jack?" A familiar, portly man with a distinguished beard has insinuated himself at Jack's side, startling him. "The way George goes on about your legendary choosiness, she must be something special."

"Oh, definitely," Jack says weakly. He *thinks* the man's name is Seymour, but he's not confident enough to say it out loud. "Quite the catch."

"Come on, lad, you have to give us more than that."

His father watches him, coolly curious, and Jack narrows his eyes, telling them, "Green eyes, dark hair, a body to die for," and imagines he can project vivid images of naked men into his father's brain.

The portly man laughs. "Brilliant. Bet she goes like a barn door in a storm, too."

"Oh, *she* does," he says through gritted teeth, eyes on his dad.

His dad slips an arm around him. "She's turned my son's whole life around, isn't that right, Jack?"

"She's special all right."

"And so tonight, Seymour, we celebrate."

"Scotches on you then, George," announces Seymour—he *knew* it—and Jack gets a second drink shoved into his hand and a few more heaps of congratulations from the gaggle of men he only knows faintly—men whose kids he used to play with during dull benefits, and men who'd flip him fifty cents with a wink when they visited his parents because they thought it was cute and uncle-y or something.

Jack eases into it, takes a nice-sized gulp of scotch and readies himself to schmooze.

Let his father believe Jack can't walk away. Let him believe in Jack's grudging and most fundamental of loyalties. Perhaps it's undeniably true to a point, pointless to argue with.

It only helps him, though, in the end, and once this is all over, his father will see what Jack's capable of. He'll watch Jack break free for real and not regret a single second of his betrayal.

His father heads toward the bar and another man takes his place, and then another, and another. Jack's surrounded by bizarre well-wishers, people who rightfully shouldn't give a fuck what he does with his life, and he marvels that had he been a different kind of person, this tailored suit and rich scotch and exuberant praise over the littlest nothing could've been all his.

Richard leans against the table in Jack's peripheral vision, staring somewhere into the middle distance, and Jack's grateful for every choice he's ever made.

Seymour starts in on his own wife, or the original version of her, the version he met thirty-five years ago, and Jack bites his tongue at the increasingly unflattering comparisons to livestock and prison guards as Seymour downs his nth drink and scratches at his thinning hair.

"I don't know if you remember this, Jack," another man drawls at him, and Jack tunes out the rest. This guy he knows by sight alone: Fredrick Duluth, an oil man moved to Broneburg from one of the southern states as well as a father to eleven kids, a few of whom Jack still sees semi-regularly in certain circles. "Lotta years ago, you can't have been more than eight, you and my little princess Martha were playing in our pool—"

He does remember this, and it makes him laugh. "And I told you I was gonna marry her."

"You did," Fredrick says indulgently.

"How is she these days? I haven't seen her in, God, must be over ten years."

"Still waiting for Mr. Right, I think."

He questions the voracity of that claim. The last time he saw Martha Duluth she had her tongue down Sol's throat. He hopes for her sake she likes men, too, because she really was Fredrick's princess and most of his very limited attention was reserved for her.

And then Fredrick shocks him by adding, "Or Mrs. Right, of course," and Jack stares at him, startled.

"You, uh—"

"Know? Course I do, I'm her daddy." It's hardly a novel concept, that a father might be supportive of his kid's personal life, but still—Jack's pretty surprised. "A girl can't help who she falls in love with."

Jack holds up his glass and smiles. "Well, I will drink to that."

And he does; bolstered by Fredrick, Jack drains the rest of his first glass and sips at his second, feeling his shoulders loosen and his demeanor become more fluid.

At no point does Richard approach him. Jack wonders if he's here simply because his father wanted it that way, another way to torture Jack, and as he spots Senator Leigh's glancing vitriolically at George and watching his son like a hawk, he thinks maybe this isn't just Jack's punishment.

What did the senator do to piss his dad off so badly? The mental gymnastics of his father's pecking order are exhausting.

Someone presses another drink into his hand and Jack manages to avoid any more questions about his pretend engagement, right up until Senator Derek Leigh seems to tire of the fruitless glaring, coming over to snidely remark, "Finally settling down, eh, Jack?"

Snidely *and* drunkenly. Jack's father smirks into his glass nearby, and Jack takes a steadying breath.

"Looks like, yeah."

"Never thought I'd see the day," Derek slurs a little. "Did you, George?"

"I knew he'd come home to roost eventually."

"Sometimes they need a push, am I right?"

"Perhaps your boy, but not mine, Derek," his father says smoothly.

"Here we go," Seymour mutters somewhere close to Jack's ear, and Jack turns his head down.

"This happen a lot?"

Seymour waves a nonchalant hand. "Oh, those two are like a couple of cats trying to piss the highest."

It gives Jack an idea, albeit a rather risky one. These people are a veritable gold mine of information, gossipy old men falling short on ways to keep themselves entertained. He can't believe it didn't occur to him before.

"Bad look, arguing with the senator," Jack chuckles. "Especially during campaign season."

"Don't worry about it." Seymour gives him a wink. "Your old man has his ways of keeping even senators in line."

"Maybe I should break it up all the same; I can't let him throw the election like this—"

Seymour touches Jack's shoulder. "I said don't worry. The campaign is a slam dunk—Derek was declawed years ago." He leans back in, whispering with so much unnecessary dramatics, "Between you and me, your father is the only thing keeping him in the Senate anyway."

"Well," Jack says slowly. "You can't blame me for being concerned."

"I can't. You're a good boy, Jack." Seymour pats him sloppily on the arm. "I can't tell you how much you look like George when he was your age, but you remind me of your mother."

He swallows thickly. "Wow, really?"

"Absolutely," Seymour says mournfully; the over-the-top emoting is frankly hilarious but Jack pangs a little all the same. "She was a fine woman, Valerie. Deserved better..." He trails off, and Jack can't decide if the sentiment is a smear against his father or her disease.

Jack assumes the latter. "I'd be careful talking like that,

Seymour."

His face pales, drained like every glass that touches his hand, and Jack bites down on a laugh. "No, no, that's not what I meant!"

He did mean Jack's father, then. Another wealthy, grown man cowed by George Preston's iron fist. Alex was right about the reach of his power, of course he was, but seeing it firsthand is actually quite extraordinary. Jack almost feels a solidarity with these men, awful as they are, because Jack grew up under that same reach, and he knows how bitter a shadow it casts.

"Senator Leigh isn't the only person my father keeps tabs on, you know," Jack tells Seymour, lowering his voice conspiratorially.

"I know that," Seymour says roughly. "Do you think I don't know that?"

Fascinating, truly. Jack pats Seymour on the arm in return, assuming he must like that kind of thing. "I love the man, I really do, but sometimes I think he's too paranoid for his own health."

Seymour's eyes go greedy-wide, his whole body leaning eagerly toward Jack. "His health is bad?"

Jack's scotch burns a bit on its way back up as he presses his snort into his fist. "His bark is worse than his bite these days. Mostly he relies on me to pick up the slack."

"That's admirable, Jack," Seymour says, very slowly.

"I'm not the hard-ass he is, though."

Jack turns back to where Derek Leigh is still glaring at his father, mostly being ignored in favor of conversation with other people. "Senator, a drink?"

Derek narrows his eyes, and Jack doesn't wait for an answer, heading for the bar. It's what his father would do, display uncompromising authority like that, and between that and the slick assurance of his suit, Jack feels almost confident enough to push some limits. Fake it and the rest will follow, apparently.

His dad bringing him here has the surprising potential to be fortuitous. Alex would be pleased, he thinks warmly.

Jack's not expecting the senator's appearance at his shoulder, leaning mirrored against the bar top while Jack orders more drinks to be brought over.

"I can get my own damn drink," he growls.

"I'm trying to be polite," Jack says smoothly.

Derek scoffs. "Polite. Is that what you call it?"

"What do you call it?"

"An insult."

He hates this man—he remembers, vividly, precisely how much he *hates* this man. The stiff bulwark of his back indifferent to Jack getting crushed, to his own son being humiliated. Richard's in here with a wedding ring forced onto his finger, and Jack suddenly can't see straight with the injustice of it.

A waiter swings out from behind the bar with a tray of drinks balanced precariously on one hand, and Jack leans his hip against the dark wood, facing down a truly old hurt.

"An insult would be me tipping that tray over your fucking head."

"And there he is." Derek sneers. "That's the nasty little boy I remember."

"The *boy*—"

"The boy who corrupted my son and almost ruined his life."

"That's funny, because if I recall, my father said the exact same thing about Richard."

Derek scoffs. "Your father doesn't know his ass from his elbow."

"Funny again," Jack drawls, "because he says the exact the same thing about you."

He watches the senator's face twist, ugly and then flushing red, and Jack's getting nowhere but damn if it doesn't feel good to be this petty. This place is like high school, he realizes, and these grown-ass adults like teenagers. It's indulgent to revert to that, air out these historical gripes with a bit of good old mudslinging.

He can suddenly see the appeal of it.

"I can't decide if you're just like him or if it's all an act," Derek says through his gritted teeth. "What are you playing at?"

"Maybe I should ask Richard the same question. That's an awfully pretty ring on his finger."

"Awfully pretty girl who put it there. And now you've got one of your own."

"I'm a lucky man," Jack sing-songs.

"You're a damn liar and a fake."

"And what concern is that to you?"

"I don't give a flying fuck about you or your father."

"Obviously," Jack snaps. "Or you'd tear him apart instead of just yapping at his heels."

He's hit a nerve, visibly. The senator's gotten lax with his public front in the years since Jack's affair with his son, clearly. "You don't have a clue what you're talking about." His words, his whole demeanor, screams like he's just outright given up. That bulwark of his back is slumped, now, and it's a satisfying demolition.

Derek slams a fist against the bar top, yelling into the crowd, "*George*," and then, "Come collect your son, you rotten old bastard," and Jack's dad pushes through with something close to panic on his face.

"What's going on here?"

"Oh, nothing," Jack jumps in with quickly. "Just talking to Senator Leigh here about politeness."

His dad looks at him curiously. "Is that right?"

"You should teach your son the meaning of the word, George," Derek snaps. "Or perhaps you already did."

And just like that they're in it again, and Jack slips away quietly, because as funny as it was the first time, it's not like he feels more much charitable toward his father than he does the senator; there's no one to root for here. Jack shouldn't have gotten into it, really, but some hurts still sting.

He finds Seymour again, planted firmly next to a tall round table with the drinks tray on. He hands Jack one on approach and Jack nods his thanks.

"Don't wade into it," Seymour tells him. "Trust me."

"It waded into me."

"You have your own issues with Derek, it seems?"

Clever of him; Seymour's been watching, too. Vultures, the lot of them. "These things tend to get passed down the line." Seymour studies him closely, and Jack quips, "Who else am I going to have to fight?"

Seymour laughs. "It's all part of the fun, my boy."

Jack tosses him a sly look. "If I point, will you tell me yes or no?"

"Sounds entertaining, go right ahead."

Jack glances around the room, knocking back some more of his scotch to stop his glass looking quite so suspiciously full.

"Okay," he says eagerly. "Him."

Seymour follows his gesture. "Bill Lescovak, position currently shaky."

He surreptitiously points again. "Him? Green shirt, balding."

"Roland Linsley, you may have to fight him."

Jack grins. "What about him?"

"That's Harold McKouen." Jack does a spit-take; he hadn't even recognized the judge, pallid and hunched as he is. "He is, so far, untouchable."

"He doesn't look well."

"No, the man is a nervous wreck these days." Seymour takes a haughty drink. "Absolutely no fun at all."

"Okay, what about him?" Jack says, directing Seymour toward the man who's spent most of the evening so far sat in a high-backed leather armchair looking bored.

"That," Seymour says with relish, "is Luca Baumann."

"Baumann," Jack repeats. "That name sounds familiar."

"Perhaps. He's notorious—if not publicly, then definitely behind closed doors."

Baumann—he can see the name in writing, exactly how it's spelled. Slanted in some kind of cursive, too, somewhere in his memories.

"Well?" Jack pushes.

It's like Seymour was just waiting for Jack to pay *more* attention to him; he's in his element here, hardly able to contain a grin as he tells Jack, "If sad old Harry is untouchable, Luca is the almighty God himself."

Jack whistles, playing up to it. "Wow, should I start making nice with him?"

"That might not be such a terrible idea. He's the kind of man everybody needs use of one day."

"What is he, a hitman?"

Seymour throws his head back and laughs uproariously, and

Jack watches him, bemused. "Oh, you are much more fun than your father."

Seems Jack doesn't get to know what Luca does, nor about the trials of Harry McKouen, now he comes to think of it. Seymour is a terrible gossip, but he's not stupid. There's a code here amongst these men, as warped as it is, and Jack's still an outsider.

He needs to feed Alex the names, see what he can dig up.

He asks Seymour for directions to the bathroom, picking his way through the increasingly drunk and rowdy crowd, the steadily climbing voices. He has no idea where his father's gone, but he makes it across the room and into the little hall to the restroom without bumping into him.

The bathroom is just as suffused with luxury as the rest of the place. Jack understands the expense of black granite and gold-plated fittings in a way that scotches and cognacs escape him. He could pay rent for a year with what this bathroom probably cost to furnish.

Thankfully, it's empty.

Jack takes out his phone.

Harold McKouen is here & more names for you: Bill Lescovak, Roland Linsley, and Luca Baumann. Last one is really familiar.

The reply comes within seconds.

I'll run them, how are you holding up?

Jack checks his stupid pleased grin in the mirror, shaking his head.

Pretty good, drunk rich guys love to gossip. I could be a pro at this stuff yet. Btw it's my engagement party, congrats?

He waits just a few seconds again, deleting the communications so far—can't forget to wipe them, he can't take the risk.

That's gonna need some explaining later, I'll be sure to pick up a gift for you though.

He wishes this wasn't so easy, this quippy back and forth that has inevitably devolved every damn time with them into blatant flirting. Jack just cannot help himself; it's like sinking into something warm and electric, so sweet and appealing but makes his hair stand on end, makes him thrum.

For reference, I'm partial to Silver Brush art supplies. Hope you've got deep pockets.

He wishes Alex wasn't so—Alex. Such a perfect fit for him in every way except the obvious, the terrifying thing he does.

Anything for you, dear. Am I allowed to say that or will your new fiancée get jealous?

Jack laughs, allowing himself that second of indulgence, and slips the phone back in his pocket before he can be tempted anymore.

Wanting is such a dangerous thing—single-minded all the way up to this point in his life and now fractured into so many threads he can't feel the end. It used to be stability and freedom he craved;

now it's something so much more complex.

He's getting ahead of himself.

Jack straightens his tie and collar, brushes his fingers through his hair, and looks utterly the role of a wealthy political progeny.

He pushes a hand against the restroom door and steps out, hears a rough voice tell him, "Time for your engagement gift," and everything suddenly goes dark.

Chapter Fifteen

He doesn't know how long he's blinded for.

Doesn't know and can't focus past trying to inhale and exhale without falling into some kind of panic attack, so much concentration to just fucking *breathe*. The air in his lungs is damp and recycled and the black bag over his head is uncompromisingly opaque.

He'd been grabbed by both arms and dragged and guided somewhere, down three sets of stairs and a hall, the opening of a stiff and creaky door and the smell of damp brickwork telling him he's probably in a basement room.

They'd placed him on a chair, tied his hands to the arms, his ankles to the legs, and then left.

And now he's left alone to wonder why, which subsequently tells him that his father has to be behind this because it's a clever trick, making Jack build it up in his head like this, his excessive imagination running rings.

It's a suffocating fear, worse than the actual suffocating, a dread palpable enough to choke on. He's fucked up somehow; his dad has known all along or Jack's been too cocky, asking too many questions up there because he thinks he's a big shot now. Someone took his phone on the way down here and he can't remember if he deleted his messages or not; if they've broken the passcode, then—

It's an endless string of thought, twisting him in tighter knots. He hadn't fought them, the people dragging his ass down here, so he had to have known on some level that he wasn't in any real danger.

It's the waiting that's the danger, though.

He waits.

Waits until the door creaks open again, Jack's whole body tensing.

"You sound scared."

It's a voice he doesn't recognize, and Jack says nothing.

"Come on, if you can't handle this you'll never make it as a Brother."

Jack breathes, "Huh?"

The bag is removed and even the low lights of the room make his eyes sting. The man standing a few feet away is the one Jack saw for a split-second before he was grabbed, someone he doesn't know at all. Only the voice is familiar; something about an engagement gift.

Maybe he's got this all wrong.

"You're in for a treat, son," the man says with a lewd grin, and then he's gone, the door left open.

"Uh, excuse me?" Jack tries awkwardly. "The hell is going on here?"

He wishes he hadn't asked, he really does. Not that it would've made a damn bit of difference.

She enters the room in a click of high heels and a cloud of rich perfume, closing the door behind her with a dainty, manicured hand.

Jack mutters, "Engagement gift," under his breath, and now he *knows* this is his father; it's got George Preston all fucking over it.

The woman turns with a smile, blonde hair pinned up in curls and her body covered up by a long black coat.

"You are a real looker," she tells him, and he stares up at her at a total loss of speech. "So what'll it be for the husband-to-be?"

"Look, I—" he starts, struggling, can't *believe* how messed up this is. "I'm a little uncomfortable here. Could you untie me, maybe?"

She takes her hands away from the lapels of her coat, looking hesitant. "There were rules."

"You can't untie me?"

She shakes her head, frowning now.

Jack tugs harder at the ropes, rattling the chair frame. "*Fuck.*" He raises his voice, knows that someone out there will hear it— straight from their lips to his dad's ears. "I'm not doing this! I have—I have a fiancée who I love very much, and I won't do this to her."

The woman backs up against the door. "He said you were game, I didn't—"

"Hey, hey," he says softly, can't quit fucking struggling, though, even though all it's doing is making his wrists sore. "It's okay, this isn't your fault." She doesn't look convinced. "*Who* said I was game?"

"The man who calls the agency; I don't know which one he is."

She surreptitiously rattles the door handle behind her back, and Jack sees her eyes go wide when she finds it locked.

Jack repeats, "Fuck," and then implores her, "Please can you untie me?"

She doesn't want to. She's locked in a room with the ropes around Jack's wrists maybe her only protection, and she's legitimately afraid.

"Look, I can see why you wouldn't, this is sketchy as hell," he reasons, "but I had nothing to do with this, I swear. I'm not gonna hurt you."

She shakes her head, tipping her face back to the ceiling and imploring it, "What the hell is going on here?"

"I guess the guys thought I'd appreciate this, but uh, like I said—fiancée." He tries out a laugh. "No offence to you. You're very beautiful."

She holds up a hand. "Okay, God, stop, *please*," she says and takes a step toward him, warning him, "I will Mace your ass if you pull something funny."

"I believe that," he tells her.

She's not half a dozen feet from him when the lock jangles and the door swings open. Some guy grabs her arm and pulls her from the room, and Jack's father steps in right past them, smooth as anything.

Jack's shouting before the door even closes. "Hey, what the hell are you doing with her?"

"Taking her away like you wanted."

"You asshole, what were you *thinking*—"

"Didn't I tell you to play along like a good boy?"

He glares up at his father's blank, *blank* face, clenched fists shifting the sore skin of his wrists against the ropes. "I'm not fucking someone on your say-so."

George pulls a stool from somewhere off to Jack's side and drags it up in front of the chair, taking a seat and leaning forward into Jack's space with his elbows on his knees.

"Is it that you can't get it up for her?" he asks lightly, like they're discussing the weather or something. "Because we have drugs for that."

Jack's face twists. "You told your pals I was engaged tonight."

"This is how we celebrate engagements."

"Even *fake ones*?" he hisses, and his father grimaces; finally, a reaction.

"Say that a little bit louder, Jack, and you won't be leaving this room at all."

Jack looks into his father's face, his eyes, the fine lines around his mouth, the cut of his jaw, and tells him, "You're *insane*. You're completely insane."

"Your phone is mostly empty, you know."

"What?"

"You're deleting your communications."

"I was—" He can't keep the stutter out of his voice, taking a shaky breath and trying to swallow down a load of spit at the same time. "I was told to; they told me to."

His father hums, blank expression again. "It's funny," he starts mildly, looking down at the floor between his knees. "I expected you to walk out tonight, after the announcement. That's what my son would've done."

Jack asks, "You wanted me to walk out?" but he knows exactly what his dad means.

"So willing," George goes on, ignoring him. "I can't figure out an acceptable why."

"Because every time I try to fight you, I lose. I don't wanna be an errand boy for criminals any more than I wanna be here, but what else am I supposed to do, huh? I can't run, you already pointed that out."

"Catch twenty-two," his father sing-songs. "It's flawless reasoning."

Jack rattles the chair. "Then why am I still tied to this thing?"

"I think you learned your reasoning skills from me, no?"

Jack scoffs, telling his father with a humorless smile, "And you wouldn't trust yourself."

George grins wolfishly. "I think you really are more like me than you'd ever dare to admit."

"Only in the ways that don't make people wanna kill me."

His father's face doesn't drop at all. "There's my Jack." He taps his chin. "What a dilemma we're in."

"What can you even do to me?"

"Make you honest, son. Make a man out of you."

"I'm not having sex with that woman," Jack says quickly. "Not willingly, and she doesn't strike me as a rapist."

"There are other ways to test a man's strength of character."

Jack's thinking lie detectors or syringes filled with sodium thiopental, both of which Jack knows nothing about the voracity of, if they'll have him gushing like a geyser. What he gets is neither of those things and much worse, and Jack may well have watched too many movies because he's seen this trick a hundred times, too.

The barrel of a revolver presses against his forehead.

"No," he says immediately. He means *you can't, you won't, there's no way—*

"I made you," his father drawls. "Now I want to know you."

Click.

Jack gasps, jerking back, frantically trying to turn his head away as far as he can get. "Oh my *God*."

"Anything you'd like to tell me, Jack?"

"No! This is insane!"

Click.

He cries out this time, half a scream. He can't—can't fucking *breathe*—

"There must be something you have to tell me," his father says so softly, how can be so fucking *Goddamn* calm.

"I don't know what you want!"

Click.

Jack's voice cracks, splitting apart. He tears the skin of wrists struggling, only faintly feels the hot burn and rush of blood, sees his staining shirt sleeves like they're not even a part of him.

It's happening. It's happening, and he's helpless against it, can't get loose, can't move, can't do a thing but look down the barrel.

"You know what I want, Jack." Calm, so damn calm. Cold, gray stare, utterly composed—Jack hates him, *hates him.*

Could Jack make it stop? Would it be worth it if his father knew the truth?

"I've told you everything, I've risked everything for you over and over—"

Click.

"—*stop it!* God*dammit!*"

Two chambers left.

"You couldn't, you couldn't kill me," Jack chokes, voice wrecked. "You're my dad, and I don't believe you could kill me any more than I could let you die."

Could a man kill his own son in cold blood? Even a man like George Preston? Jack thinks no, thinks it so utterly, so necessary and fundamental, that he can't tell if the shock's letting him sink into denial or not.

"What. Aren't. You. Telling. Me."

Jack glares him right in the eye, trembling in every muscle, chest jerking with every breath. "Nothing."

His father stares back, seconds, hours, fucking days in that stare.

Click.

Jack groans, dipping his head, shaking it. Tears fall into his lap; he grits his teeth around making more noise.

If he tells the truth, they're fucked. There's no going back. If his father is perfectly willing to put a bullet in him for not talking, it stands to reason nothing will change once Jack blabs. He has nothing to gain from talking, not a damn thing, and even if he did—

Jack doesn't know that he would.

If his father's bluffing—and he *is*, he must be—then Jack will just have to call it.

He looks up—wants to be looking his father in the eye if he is, in fact, about to die. Wants his defiance to be the last thing ever passed between them.

"Pull the trigger, you bastard, go on."

His father smiles.

Click.

Silence.

Jack stares, frozen, unblinking, but his dad just keeps on smiling.

"Impressive," he quips.

He stands, dragging the stool back to the corner of the room, and Jack stares straight ahead, at the absence his father and his gun left behind.

The ropes on one wrist start to loosen, and he thinks an age must've passed, looking down to see his father finally untying him. He drags a hand free, works on the other, then his ankles, and then he stands, staggers, almost falls the hell down, but he still swings for his dad's face, fuck it.

His fist hits against a jaw, glancing off; Jack's uncoordinated and burning with it, everything. Hot with rage and clumsy with relief.

His father lashes back, clocking Jack on the cheekbone, and then he laughs, stepping backwards toward the door.

"That's the spirit, Jack. Perhaps you will make a good Brother after all."

"A Brother," Jack snaps, hard but a little wobbly. "Fuck you."

"I wouldn't turn your nose up at this, son. You fit in remarkably well with those people upstairs."

"It's an act."

"You think even one of those pricks up there isn't acting?"

Jack needs to get the hell out of here. "I'm walking out right now, and you're not gonna stop me."

"So long as you're back by tomorrow." His father shrugs, opening the door and leaving it that way. "There's a situation needs dealing with after all."

"Where's my phone?"

"Oh, *that's* where you're going." His father sticks his head out into the hall and gestures for someone. "Your green-eyed boy."

Jack flinches.

"I'm presuming he's whoever *A* is." Someone appears in the doorway, handing George a phone, which he then tosses across the room to Jack. "Stay off the radar. I've got better things to do than clean up after you tonight."

Jack's cheek starts to throb. He clutches the phone white-knuckle tight and storms out of the room before anyone can stop him, before his father can scrutinize the look on his face.

He climbs the stairs he was manhandled down, finds signs leading to the exit, and gets back to the lobby. He can't imagine the state he looks right now, but the man in red still beaming behind the front desk doesn't seem at all surprised by it, which Jack thinks says a lot about this place.

"Call me a cab, please," he says tightly.

"Of course, sir. To where?"

"The Mile. Put it on my father's account."

He doesn't stick around to make small talk, spilling out down the front steps and striding out to the road before he gives into the crippling demands of his body, doubles over and dry-heaves.

It hurts, his stomach clenches violently, but nothing comes up despite the booze.

Jack fumbles with both his phone and his collar buttons, ripping off and pocketing his tie and squinting at the cell screen against the blurring in his eyes.

The incriminating messages are gone. Gone, and Jack can actually pull in a breath that doesn't taste like bile.

The ones left behind are nothing but idle flirting and he remembers, now that he can actually think back, deleting the worst of them in the bathroom.

His cab slides up beside him, and he throws himself straight into it, wanting to get as far away from this fucked up place as humanly possible. He slams the door behind him, tipping his head back against the seat and letting the drift of movement, the gaining distance, attempt to lull him.

He doesn't think he'll be followed tonight, but he's taking no chances by coming here, pulling up at a late-night coffee place at the head of the bustling Mile. The driver will report back to the lodge, most likely, but Jack intends to be long disappeared into the lights and bodies by then.

Once the car pulls away, Jack momentarily leans back against the wall outside, overcome for a second with a dizzying frailty.

Because, *God,* he just had a gun in his face, an unloaded gun, but there were odds stacked against him. His father sat there while Jack struggled and fretted and just—smiled. It's unimaginable, impossible to quantify. He stares blindly into the sky and can't with a head full of static and self-reproach.

He needs to walk. He needs Alex like a bandage over an open wound.

It's beautifully, predictably crowded, and Jack brings the phone eagerly to his ear, just two rings before Alex answers.

"Hey."

Now he hears Alex's voice, he chokes, has to squeeze his eyes shut against the rush of desperation. "Hey, I'm out."

"Is everything all right?"

"Yeah." Jack rubs a hand over his face, wincing at the heated bruise on his cheek. "No. I don't know. Can you come meet me?"

"Jack, are you okay?"

"Fine, just come, please," Jack begs. "I'll be outside the Irish bar on the Mile."

Alex tells him, "I'll be there as soon as I can," with an impenetrable conviction.

They hang up, Jack grudgingly, but Alex sounds like he's already on the move before the call even disconnects.

He sets himself to walking off his tide-like adrenaline, the slippery to-and-fro of his energy reserves. He's exhausted but stopping, missing the reverberation of movement, feels unthinkable. Every step is still shaky with uncertainty; he just doesn't know where he stands anywhere, always on uneven ground—*don't you forget it.*

He'll never win. If he puts his father away for the rest of his life, there will be no escaping this feeling.

Jack reaches the bar after some indeterminate time, losing track of the minutes ticking by, and leans against the cold brickwork, watching the people mill past.

It's like carrying a disease in the middle of a healthy crowd. Jack feels invisibly toxic, weighted down by a corrosive filth. He probably looks like some drunk stockbroker in a nice suit slumming down here with the little people, like he got in a bar fight and got asked to cool his head, and he sees the people walking by the exact same way; just the shell of them, without their experiences and upheavals.

Even in all the crowd, Alex is magnetic to Jack.

The opposite of every ordinary person, he's a beacon at two-hundred yards, striding toward Jack quickly in his jeans and leather jacket, reflecting red, then yellow, then blue, as he passes under the spilling bar lights.

Instantly, he demands, "What happened?"

"I'm fine," Jack croaks, and he can't seem to move himself off the wall, making his point questionable. "I'm okay, I swear."

He's telling Alex, but he's telling himself, too, and it feels more true now that he has an anchor here to hold to.

"Oh, yeah, you totally seem it."

Jack laughs wetly. "Well, I'm overdramatic, you must've realized that by now."

Alex steps close to him, frowning. He raises a hand, and Jack holds his breath for it, but it never touches, just lingers in his eyeline before Alex drops it. Could've been for the bruise on his face; could've been for Jack himself.

"Please tell me what happened."

"Thought I was a goner." Jack sniffs. "Well, maybe a goner. I don't even know what I was thinking."

"Did he figure you out?"

"No, I got lucky," he says and then scoffs. "Lucky."

"Jack—"

Jack shakes his head minutely. "Can we go somewhere?"

Alex hesitates a few seconds and then nods. "Sure. I'm parked close to here."

And then he does something Jack doesn't expect: minutely extends his arm with his palm flat out as an offering.

Jack swallows, reaches out and barely hooks their fingertips together, and Alex uses it to gently draw him away from the wall, backing up to get Jack walking forward.

Alex slowly tangles their fingers together, and then they're moving, side by side, through the throng, breathing in the smell of spirits and perfumes and cigarette smoke.

They don't speak on the short walk. It's enough right now for

Jack to just feel safe, even when he's all but lost the meaning of the word.

Alex drives a sweet car, a thing Jack hadn't had the concentration to notice until now. It's black, which he knew, but it's subtly seductive, not overstated at all. Alex to a T, really, and Jack climbs in feeling deceptively at home.

"You obviously get paid too much," he quips hoarsely, and Alex smirks.

They pull away from the plaza, and now that Jack's started talking, now he's in flight, it's much easier to carry on.

He watches the scenery roll past the window and tells Alex the whole sordid story from beginning to harrowing end, leaving it behind in a trail with the eaten-up miles.

Chapter Sixteen

Jack doesn't specify a location, and Alex seems to take that as green to go wherever the road takes him.

They drive away from the Mile. The lights and people thin as the darkness and sleeping suburbs swell. Jack hasn't driven in years, and he couldn't say where they were exactly. Doesn't much care, either.

Alex takes them up the winding roads, higher into the hills where the stars become brighter than the distant city center, and Jack watches nature start to encroach on the suburbia, trees whipping past instead of idyllic houses and acres of marshland that surrounds the west part of Broneburg.

He thinks they're at the highest point when Alex slows the car. He turns them in to an overlook, just a patch of dried-down mud between thickets of trees, the real road left far behind. Jack climbs out without a word, walking to the edge. The hill drops off six or so feet from the car front, and the city's a scale of gray underneath, dark blending up to light the further out it goes.

It's quite the gift, this view.

He turns at the sound of Alex's footsteps in the sparse grass and sees him taking a seat, perched on the hood of the car. They're rather striking in the dense silence, wind inexplicably dropped down to nothing. Jack slips off his jacket, tossing it over a low branch, and rolls up his shirtsleeves, air warmly settling on his forearms and throat, the bits of him exposed.

Alex, unmistakably, looks him up and down. Up, down and away, with a shudder of breath.

"How's your face?"

Jack touches a finger to the sore bit of skin. "I got him back."

"Not hard enough."

"Well that's the point of what we're doing."

Alex looks at him again, darker this time, harder to tell what he's thinking. "Sure."

"Are you pissed at me or something?" Jack snaps.

"No," Alex says firmly, no room for doubt there.

"Then—" Jack stops. Alex is pissed, sure, but Jack knows where it's directed, and that—that makes it personal again, doesn't it? Alex's inability to be objective or thick-skinned where Jack's concerned. He realizes he's just trying to make Alex admit it out loud all over again, contrary to the lines drawn. All Jack can think about is stepping over them, trampling them into smudges. "Okay."

Alex winces, looking down at the ground between his knees. "How do you feel about going back to him after this?"

"Honestly, I don't know."

"A bullet could still put him down just as thoroughly." Alex's hands curl over the front of the hood. Jack imagines him with a weapon to hold instead, the swift hand of justice, and his throat flutters around the visual. "All you'd have to do is get him somewhere I could see him."

Jack takes a shaky breath. "That wasn't part of the deal."

"Extenuating circumstances."

"Nothing has changed," Jack stresses. "I'm bringing down the son of a bitch, alive. It's the only way, you know that."

"Why do you want him to live so much?" Alex snaps, staring up, mouth parted.

"Decades of corruption?" Jack parrots back at him, words right out of Alex's own mouth. "Retrials? Disbarrings? Ringing any bells for you?"

"Why do *you* want him to live so much?"

"Because! Because he's all I got left of my family and," Jack stutters, "and because I want him to look me in the eye and *know* it was me who destroyed him." He takes a hard breath. "And what about you? You act like the man killed your puppy or something!"

Alex's expression does something dangerous; Jack's heart flinches but he takes a contrary step forward all the same.

"Tell me," and then, "*please*, Alex, please tell me."

"It's my reason for doing what I do," Alex says softly, at odds with the set of his jaw. "I can't make it your reason too."

"I'm not that easily manipulated, Alex, come on."

Alex shuts his eyes, shaking his head. Jack thinks he's been gently dismissed, not sure if he's ready to let it drop or not, but then Alex pats the car hood beside him, an invitation Jack carefully takes.

He nudges their shoulders together a little; he's here, he's here for anything Alex thinks he has to hide. From this vantage he can see the city again, its bright central web of power and faded edges.

"I enlisted right outta high school," Alex begins. "My family was broke; it seemed like the right thing to do. Turned out I was good at it, made it to Sergeant, and the pay was nice. It helped out my folks. I didn't wanna do it forever, but I'd caught someone's eye, kept telling me he had big things in store for me. It was exciting, I was twenty-four, y'know?" He goes quiet, stretch of silence pulling taut. "And then my dad was shot and killed."

Jack swallows, breathes, "Oh my God."

"He was just at work," Alex says with a humorless snort. "Some dumb kids jacked an expensive car at gunpoint and went on a joyride, and it turned into a city-wide police chase."

Jack waits out another silence. Feels like Alex is carving this story out in manageable fragments of a difficult whole.

"Turned out the kid with the gun was Leonard Rathbone's son."

No—

Jack speaks hoarsely. "My dad's twenty-ten campaign manager."

"The kid walked."

Jack starts, "Because," and can't finish that sentence; he's utterly grateful that Alex doesn't finish it for him.

"I knew it was sketchy, and I pried into things I shouldn't have. I got involved when I shoulda stayed away."

Same story, different verse, and Alex *said*, he said this isn't what he wanted for Jack.

"But David protected me," Alex goes on. "Gave me— opportunities. They felt like opportunities. I was so pissed off all the time; he put me through special training and told me if I could prove myself, I'd get a crack at the assholes who'd destroyed my family."

David, Alex's mystery *sort of* recruiter.

David, who he'd reported back to with a plea for Jack's involvement and safety.

"Your father's been his personal vendetta for years." Alex looks down and huffs a laugh. "You ever have someone you wish you'd never—"

"Yeah." Jack nudges him again. "Yeah, I do."

"I think I owe him, but it's hard to tell these days."

Owe him for using your father's death to groom you into a dangerous job? Jack doesn't say it, though, because there's some potentially uncomfortable parallels here, and Alex already thinks the worst of himself over Jack being thrown to the wolves.

"But I got my chance, and I blew it."

"I'm your second chance," Jack says softly.

Alex slants him a look. "Amongst other things." His mouth is very close; it's a real struggle to look away from it.

He probably shouldn't have said it, but Jack shouldn't have pushed, and now they're in it too far, too close. Jack's going to kiss him, and Alex knows he is, and it's everything Jack was trying to avoid but had absolutely no hope of doing so. He single-mindedly wants Alex's mouth under him so fucking *bad* he can feel it in his spine, the curve of it yearning forward.

Jack bites down on his lip, sucks it into his mouth. Alex starts, "God, if you want to, just—" and doesn't get to finish before Jack's on him, dry and hard at first because he's trying to prove some inexplicable point, and then wetly sucking on Alex's bottom lip, parting him up and sliding his tongue inside.

Alex grabs the back of his shirt, fingers hooked over the starchy collar, and somewhere, distantly, his phone rings.

Rings and rings, but Jack's all caught up, until he feels Alex kind of snap out of it.

"Shit. *Shit.*"

Jack's pressed against air suddenly like a dousing of cold water, and Alex stands, fumbling comically with his pocket, before he brings the phone up.

He clears his throat, giving Jack a sheepish look. "Yeah?"

Jack blows out a laugh, rubbing a hand over his face, *God*, what a cock-block; he doesn't know if he's relieved or not. Seems appropriate, though, that they should be startled out of almost fucking by a big old reality check.

"Danny, that's great, hold on." Alex gestures to get Jack's attention. "Details on your rich guys."

"Hit me."

Alex repeats what he's told down the phone: "William Lescovak, stock broker; Mr. Lisley, head psychiatrist at Broneburg Penitentiary; and Luca Baumann—" Alex pauses, concentrating, and then tells Jack, "Daddy's a major Swiss banker, and he himself is the CEO of P.B. Holdings here in the US."

"The bank?" Jack asks.

"Yeah. Thanks, Danny, I'll get back to you."

"When one of the men told me his name, I remembered seeing it somewhere."

"Plenty of money folks do business with him. Your father probably does."

"It was on his desk, the signature on a piece of paper, um, an access ticket or something," Jack remembers, clearly now. "I saw it when my dad was threatening me with that file."

"An access ticket?" Alex asks, like it means something.

"Pretty sure that's what it said."

"Hold up." Alex flicks through his phone still in his hand, bringing it back up to his ear. "Danny? I need you to look into something else for me, check if the Broneburg branch of P.B. Holdings has a safe deposit system."

Jack watches him unabashedly, his hand curled loose around his cell, the nail of his third finger caught between his teeth. He glances down at Jack, flushing at the scrutiny, and Jack sees that up-and-down glance again, the tiny dip of his throat as he looks away.

He thanks the person down the line again and tucks his phone back into his pocket. "Ever known your father to have a key that never seemed to go with anything, the house, the car, y'know?"

"He's kept a weird little double-sided silver one inside his wallet ever since I was a kid," Jack tells him; he was fascinated by that key when he was younger.

"Sounds like a safe deposit key to me." Alex picks up a pace, fingers pinching at his bottom lip. "Access tickets can be used by a box holder for one trip to the vault. It'd be signed by both people in possession of a key—your father and whoever he was renting the box from."

Jack stands; Alex's nervous energy is bleeding into him. "So you're thinking he signed my file out from a safe deposit box?"

"It's worth checking out."

"Okay, so how can I prove it?" Alex quits pacing, turning to look at Jack. He huffs a dry little laugh, and Jack asks him, "What?"

"Nothing." Alex shakes his head. "I need you to get whatever it is he's blackmailing Kalhoff with and the access ticket he used to sign it out." He slumps a little, returning to his perch on the car hood with a heavy sigh. "That's if my theory's on the money, anyway. And if it is, without something that concrete, a warrant for a vault like that is impossible, and I doubt he just keeps those tickets lying around the house."

"He probably shreds them."

"Bingo."

"No offence or anything, but why does the government even need a warrant?"

"Banks are notoriously protective of their biggest clients. P.B Holdings would fight us to the death; the whole operation would be at risk. No, it has to be legit, and once you've got the evidence, knowing your father's connections, it has to be *immediate*—give him and Baumann no time to get wind and react."

Jack looks down at him for a handful of seconds. He's got that edgy feeling again, a humming in his skin, heart lightly fluttering in his chest.

"Get the evidence, get the ticket, no problem," he says softly.

"The pressure's already on your father, just—turn it up. Make him desperate. I believe in you, Jack, and I'm not just saying that because of how I feel about you."

Jack takes a step forward, unnecessarily close again. "Yeah?"

"You're tenacious as hell and—and stubborn, and reckless, and stupidly ballsy—"

"Is this you complimenting me?" Jack grins.

"And you look smoking hot in a suit."

Jack tips Alex's chin back, leaning low, murmuring against his mouth, "S'better."

Feels like falling, completely, helplessly inevitable. Jack's got a million things to think about, but right now, in this fleeting break in the clouds, this one is his affirmation.

Alex reaches out like it's his, too.

He fists both hands into Jack's shirt to slowly untuck it. "God, this *suit*." He catches Jack's bottom lip between both his own, fingers under Jack's shirt, moving down to his fly. "Let me suck your dick in it."

"*Jesus*." Jack rolls his forehead against Alex's, going hoarse. "Warn a guy."

Alex pops the button of his black pants, molding his hand to the shape of Jack's dick getting hard through the smooth material. His hand first and then he's ducking, and Jack has to stand straight and steady himself against the car hood with one knee as Alex mouths a damp line against him.

It's warm, wet, torturously not enough, but Jack fists a shaky hand into Alex's hair and presses him there all the same, teasing lips and tongue just faint sensations through the layers. Jack groans like he's getting deepthroated, crazy gone already.

"It's not even been twenty-four hours since I last fucked you," he points out, a cursory observation to himself more than for Alex.

Alex hums a spine-tingling agreement against his cock, fingers pinched and tugging around his zipper. He rubs his nose into the skin above Jack's waistband, presses a bunch of sloppy kisses there as he grinds an open palm against Jack's dick, peeling away the layers of material until warm, damp air hits him.

Even though he's watching, Jack isn't prepared for the feeling of Alex's lips on his cock. It takes everything not to move, buck into it, fucking lose himself, but there's something about Alex teasing him out like this that's addictively toe-curling.

Jack tries to speak, "So suits, huh?" The head of his dick is resting against Alex's bottom lip as he looks up—*fuck*. He runs a hand up Jack's stomach, beneath the shirt, and gives him a smirk that's all in the eyes. "That a G-man thing?"

He slowly wraps a hand around Jack's cock, every finger pressing individually in, rubbing arcs and circles with his thumb. "Maybe I gotta thing about powerful men."

"How about the sons of powerful men?"

Alex rakes his fingernails against Jack's chest, making him twitch and sink both hands through Alex's soft hair. "You got no idea, do you?" He licks a hot line up the underside of Jack's cock, wetting it for the sluggish slide of his hand. "First time we met you had me restrained in your fucking lap."

Jack groans. "Man, that was crazy." This—this is crazy, Alex's breath hitting his dick, the gritty feel of his fingers and the low realness of his voice.

"You didn't run, you *haven't* run, Jack—" He sounds, *God*, so fucking needy, so close to the breaking point of blowing Jack's mind. "You have no idea how powerful you are." He grins, blindingly, lazily drawling, "I was not prepared for you."

Jack huffs, thumbing the corner of Alex's mouth. "Ditto."

Alex catches Jack's thumb between his teeth. "Yeah, c'mon, give it to me."

Jack bats his hand away, stroking his own dick, can't believe how hard he aches. Alex's hands curl around his hips, palm the base of his back, and Jack presses the head of his cock between Alex's lips, onto the softness of his tongue, feel of him opening up to eagerly accommodate.

His cheeks are hollowed, bones sharply defined in the dark. His eyes flutter, his throat too; Jack feeds him his whole cock, nestled unbearably deep. He doesn't know where to touch so his fingers roam, Alex's hair, his bottom lip, his jaw.

He moves minutely, fucks his own mouth with Jack's dick, barely room for air or sense, and Jack stands and takes it, trembling. All he can do is hold on until he very quickly can't anymore, until the heat and merciless sensation is too much, and he moans on a breath, "Alex, I'm gonna come, so fucking hard," because, *fuck*, his balls are aching, his dick feels wired.

Alex hums. He *swallows*. Jack shoots right in his throat, out of control and fisting a hand in Alex's hair hard enough to break roots. He does come hard, voice cracking on a shattered cry, vision blurring and stomach muscles tensing.

Alex eases off him, wiping his mouth with the back of his

hand, and Jack can barely stop shaking, fastening himself back into his fucking expensive suit with unsteady fingers. He feels like he should be tossing Alex some bills or something, the whole thing just so deliciously sordid, and he says it out loud, still delirious.

Alex laughs, swollen mouth and looking absolutely delighted with himself. He's hard in his jeans. Jack's gonna fix that once he's collected his wits.

"Maybe I'll keep the suit," he says with a grin.

"You fucking better."

"Wait, hold on." He grabs up his suit jacket and throws it casually over his shoulder, ludicrously posing. "How about now."

"Oh, baby," Alex deadpans. "You're workin' it."

Jack laughs; it feels so good to laugh, and Alex bites at his bottom lip, reaching out. "C'mere."

Jack does, hopelessly hooked, why fight it? It didn't make things any clearer, didn't make Jack magically stop wanting. There's an end to this chaos right on the horizon, and Alex—he's standing on the other side of it, Jack's sure of that now.

"Let's head back to the apartment, huh?" Alex suggests softly.

Jack glances down at the stark line of Alex's cock. "Maybe I should drive."

"Well, I am very big on road safety." He drags himself to standing by a hand in Jack's shirt, all of him sliding up against Jack's front. "How're you at handling a stick?"

Jack snorts, arms sliding tight around Alex's middle. "Like

you need to ask."

"Keys are in my front pocket."

When Jack kisses him, it puts the halt on everything; he can't imagine having anywhere better to be, anything more important to be doing. The keys are in Alex's pocket. The evidence is within Jack's reach. The fall of his father is on the horizon.

And in Jack's arms is the man who put all the wheels in motion, who gave him the tools to save himself, save them both.

Chapter Seventeen

After a few scant hours of sleep, Jack finds himself shaken awake by a youngish boy he doesn't recognize.

It's an abrupt jolt from the kind of short, tossing sleep that does more harm than good, and he sits up, sharply awake and vision oversaturated, eyes dry and stingy.

"Sorry, sir," the boy says, and Jack frowns at him. "Mr. Preston sent me to wake you."

"What time is it?"

"Nine thirty."

Jack falls back into his pillow. "No. No way. Tell Mr. Preston he can wait another six hours."

Has his dad even slept? God, his batteries are tireless. Alex dropped Jack off outside the community at five AM, and his father wasn't even home yet.

"I can't, um, really do that, sir."

Jack gestures vaguely. "No, you don't have to, just tell him I'll be down in a minute."

He hears the door click shut and says a pitiful goodbye to anything resembling rest, swinging himself out of bed to open the vertical blinds, looking right into the eye of another storm threatening the city. His view is of the river, and it's uneasy, gray, and quickly streaming by. Even the vast greenery is dull, a rainy olive color touching everything.

Jack heads for the shower to scald himself a while, burn out the colder memories from last night.

Now he has to look his father in the eye, right after George threatened his own storm.

"You look awful," is the way his father greets him in the kitchen. Sitting at the breakfast bar with a newspaper spread open in front of him, he looks the picture of alertness. Only the faint whiff of hard liquor in the air gives him away.

"You don't." Jack pours a coffee from the pot, leaning his back against the counter. "Whose blood are you sucking?"

"You're not still in a mood about last night, are you?"

He grips his cup, white-knuckled. He's making it worse by being here, he knows that; crawling back even after having a revolver shoved in his face. If his father wasn't already disturbingly enamored with the idea that Jack was a broken puppy limping back to its master, he's got to be convinced now.

Egotistic men will always be convinced of their own allure. His father's ego is his biggest downfall, the only chink in his armor Jack has to exploit.

It doesn't much sound like his father gives a crap whether Jack's *in a mood* or not, so Jack ignores him. "I'm up," he announces dryly. "What was so important that I had to be?"

His father narrows his eyes, taking a deep breath. "You know what's so important. I need your help."

Jack spills hot coffee onto the kitchen floorboards, cup in his hand slipping. He fumbles with himself, slamming the mug down onto the counter. "Could you say that again please?"

"No."

It was worth a try.

"Either I'm being conned, or the next couple of days influence whether I live or die, and I'd rather like to stay the former." His father speaks in familiar clipped tones, but his demeanor is twitchy, that dreaded brand of unpredictability that Jack's honestly afraid of and now even more so. "I can't put together a fast or safe enough means to neutralize the threat in that time, so my only option is to *buy* time."

"What are you gonna do?"

"Leave the country for a while. I'll test that bastard's bluff."

"*What?*" Jack yelps. "You—you're in the middle of a reelection campaign, you can't just go on vacation."

"Jack," his father snaps. "I will not die or be humiliated at the hands of a glorified gang leader, or anyone else for that matter. You're to tell whichever of Kalhoff's people you're in contact with that I left before you got up this morning and that you have no idea where I went."

"You think they're not gonna take it out on me, then?"

"They still need you," George says dismissively. "You proved yourself worth a damn with a gun to your head; I—trust you to handle this."

Again, Jack's body involuntarily reacts. He can't help it— waiting for almost thirty years to hear sentiments like this from his father's mouth is a very powerful poison. Jack won't be leeched of it so quickly. He wears the broken puppy shtick a little too well.

"Yesterday you didn't trust anyone!"

"Yesterday was yesterday."

What rhetorical bullshit. Jack fumes. He can't believe he didn't see this coming.

"What about the interview with the Review? It's supposed to be tonight."

"Suzanne can vouch for my disappearance when she arrives."

"This is giving up," Jack says roughly. "This is you *running away*."

His father slams a fist down on the counter top, his stool screaming across the floorboards as he stands. "This is me surviving."

"You're getting pushed out of your own city by an asshole on a power trip."

Jack is—actually upset. Because of the potential for failure, yes, but more than that—because George Preston never gives up on anything. Amoral and cruel and power-mad, all of that, but Jack's father has never displayed an ounce of backing down. It's not like he had this man on a pedestal, but Jack's always considered his father's ruthless tenacity one of his few virtues, and now that's just another thing unanchored.

"What would you suggest I do, Jack?"

Asking for advice from Jack of all people; sticking a revolver in his son's face sure has changed his perspective.

"Bargain."

"*Bargain.*"

"Let me make a deal." Jack steadies himself. "Give him whatever you've got on him."

"I will not bargain with scum like him and his people."

"No, you'll turn tail and run for the hills just like he did."

The stool goes clattering to the floor, fully thrown by his dad's outburst. "I am not begging for my life like a scared child!"

"No, I am!" Jack shouts. "You'll have to deal with him at some point. You can't go on the run forever."

"We're done talking, Jack." The split-second fury is gone; his father is again coolly composed. "This wasn't a negotiation—this was a courtesy."

They're so far away from files and safe deposit keys that Jack's lost the plot entirely, scrabbling to climb back aboard. His father is leaving the room to go pack his fucking bags, and Jack's still glaring at the space he left behind, the toppled kitchen stool and the open Financial Times.

Think fast. Faster than that.

He grips his phone in his pocket, fingering the buttons and jolting himself into action.

Jack quickly jogs through the house, rolling through the idea, seeing the wide stretch of Boyce's back before he sees his father.

"His security is too tight, it's been impossible, he's paranoid," Jack says, clearly, into his phone. "All you need is the evidence on Kalhoff." His dad shoves his way around Boyce, staring at Jack wide-eyed, both of them standing at one head of the dining table. "And *I have it*."

His father mouths, "Jack," at him sharply.

"We'll call it half the payment for a smaller job," Jack goes on. "Yes, I still expect to be paid. What d'you think this is, charity?"

Boyce is deftly dismissed from the dining room, and Jack's body involuntarily tenses, steeling for an attack of some kind.

"I understand, you need to see it before you get back to Kalhoff." Jack cringes; it sounds so damn obvious, his father's going to rumble him any second now. "I can get it to you by tonight. My father never finds out, okay? That's the condition."

He leaves the phone where it is for another half a minute or so, heart like a gong under his ribs. His father's form is a pillar of cold fury, absolute outrage, but also temperance. He's staying his hand—he might even be a little hooked.

Jack slips the phone back into his pocket on that prayer alone, staring down his father like a challenge.

"You had no damn right," he says, deceptively soft.

"You can still run, forfeit your entire campaign," Jack shrugs. "I'm not stopping you."

"You have *undermined me*—"

"I've given you options! Take the right one, for God's sake." Jack's voice cracks. "Don't abandon me to these people, don't you dare."

It's like the rug's been pulled out. His father's shoulders drop, his whole body slumps. He leans against a chair-back wearily—and weary is a good description; the toll these past weeks have taken on him finally, starkly, visible in every fallen line of his face.

"You get one chance," he says flatly. "The slightest sign of trouble and I'm gone, you can even—come with me, if you want."

Very slowly, Jack tells him, "That is quite an offer."

"If you really can get the wolves off my back, maybe we'll talk about some more."

"I don't think so." Jack sneers. "I'll never change who I am for you."

His father tilts his head curiously. "Perhaps you never needed to." He turns, starts to leave the room, and Jack's stomach feels iced, crystallized with cold. Over his shoulder, his dad tells him, "I'm going to crush Kalhoff, make no mistake," and then he's gone, Jack still suffering quietly in his wake.

Okay. *Okay.* He tips his head back, scrubs both hands over his face.

Substituting Kalhoff for Alex and the actual culprits of this operation, Jack feels fucking queasy.

Even at the very end, irreparably damned, Jack thinks his dad could make good on that vow. He's like the storm lurking outside, swirling silently and then spitting rain and lightning in its fury.

Jack hears his father climb the stairs and, on a reckless hunch, heads out to check where Boyce is.

In the hall, leaning against Jack's mother's old Victorian liquor cabinet. His father is upstairs alone and as tempted as Jack is to tell Boyce off for leaning all over the family antiques, there's a bigger temptation.

What if they were wrong about the deposit box? What if all that stuff is right here in the summer house?

Jack heads upstairs quietly, faking a big yawn for Boyce, and listens hard for any sound.

There's a voice coming from the master bedroom, very soft and only faintly audible. Jack creeps closer, feeling *again* like a fucking Hardy Boy, until he can make out the words.

"—no it has to be today, it has to be soon. Yes. I'll be over in an hour. Thank you, Luca."

Jack darts back in a panic, but his dad seems to be staying put and not immediately coming out this way. Jack creeps back to his room, pulling out the phone for real this time and telling Alex: *He was on the phone to Baumann asking to see him, think we're in business.*

Alex replies quickly: *Bingo.*

Meet me in the 7/11 parking lot on Laurel Street at eight?
Sure thing x

Jack stares blankly at the little *x*. It looks like an afterthought, such a casual little thing, and that thought is as revitalizing as the kiss itself. It's a window to the future, he hopes, and a future that Jack is molding right now, as he lives and breathes.

It's too damn early, and Jack's still fuzzy from the lack of sleep, but he's wired, determined. He has a whole nerve-wracking day to while away, and he'd better get started before he can fall back into the trap of overthought.

He changes into a T-shirt and some sweats and decides to run before the rain starts, while it's still mid-morning cool. Instinctively, Jack tenses past security on the porch, expecting to be stopped, but his lockdown days are over it seems, the freedom to walk away completely alone a strange novelty.

He takes the woods rather than the main road, the rich peppery smell and privacy appealing to his full head. Jack pounds the hard dirt, whipping past the trees and nettle bushes, pushing himself, he knows, but it feels good to ache like this, a clean ache.

Jack used to run to clear his head, but that'd take an ice pick lobotomy right now. Instead he tries to sift it, find some order in his thoughts.

He's managed well so far, and what he has left to do seems like nothing in comparison, but he's learned by now not to take anything at face value; there are no givens in this atmosphere of lies and betrayal, no predictability.

After tonight, who knows? A press explosion, a nesting doll of investigations with Jack right at the center. His face will be everywhere, most likely, and then his life story shortly afterwards, everything his father's tried for years to keep hushed up.

And then there'd be Alex. His face in the papers right next to Jack with a sordid story to boot, what a thought. Jack's got no doubt Alex will be there every step of the way if Jack lets him, and so the future boils down to that, framing itself around the man he thinks, inexplicably, he might be in love with.

He always did fall hard and fast.

Jack runs himself inside out, seeing stars and doubled over right at the edge of the community wall. He leans against it with a hand, cool white bricks smooth under his palm and covered over by moody clouds.

It's all good and well imagining the after; Jack has to get through the now first.

He walks slowly back to the house, hair damp at the back of his neck, the wind picking up. His father is already leaving as he gets halfway up the driveway.

"I'll be a few hours," he tells Jack, climbing into a waiting car with Boyce. Jack doesn't ask where he's going, doesn't need to.

That's it now: wheels in motion.

Jack eats just enough to head off his shakes, stomach starting to slowly churn, whole body growing heavier with a kind of inevitable dread. He tries to read, staring at the same page of People magazine for fifteen minutes—Jack didn't know Justin Timberlake had a kid, clearly his grasp of current events is slipping—and giving up, pacing like he always does instead.

His father's car pulls up an hour and a half after it left.

Jack's lungs can't seem to get enough air.

If he doesn't have the access ticket, the proof Alex needs to link the blackmail goods to the bank, Jack doesn't know if this will even be worth a damn.

"Dad," Jack greets him with, trying to look nonchalant on the sofa with the magazine back in his lap.

In one of his father's hands is a briefcase.

His father nods a terse hello, passing through the sitting room and into the dining room, closing the door behind him.

Fuck.

Boyce, at least, seems to have been left back out in the hall again. Jack cracks his knuckles, takes a few breaths, and knocks on the dining room door.

"What is it?"

He pushes it open slowly enough to stop if he's yelled at. "Eight PM at the 7-Eleven on Laurel Street, used to be that art supply shop, remember?"

"I remember." His father stands, framed by the gloom of the window. He has the briefcase poised open, both hands tightly gripping the lid. "Anything else?"

"Wondered if you wanted lunch."

"I could use something a little harder than lunch," he drawls, and Jack huffs a laugh.

"Yeah, me too." Jack hovers awkwardly but he supposes that's okay, given the circumstances. He glances very obviously down at the case. "Is that it?"

His father hesitates, eyes flitting between Jack and whatever's in there, eventually pulling out a manila folder similar to the one he had on Jack, only much thicker. His demeanor is stiff, like holding the thing is uncomfortable.

"Every incriminating thing on a man who should rightfully be behind bars," Jack says softly.

"Don't start moralizing, Jack, I'm not in the mood."

Jack holds up his hands. "I'm not, it's just—fascinating. You musta had him wrapped around your little finger."

And it is fascinating, Jack's not lying. He thinks it must show because his father raises a curious eyebrow. "Wrapping men around your little finger fascinates you, does it?"

Jack rolls his eyes. "Dad."

"It's all about power, son. Taking it, owning it, never giving an inch. Surely you understand that—it's what you're doing right now."

"Helping someone isn't about having power over them."

His father smirks. "You keep telling yourself that. Once you figure it out, perhaps we can finally talk like men."

Jack folds his arms, leaning back against the wall. "You know," he starts drawlingly, "Boyce sure does hang around mom's old liquor cabinet a lot."

His father's smirk gets wider. "Does he now?"

"Every time I pass through the hall, in fact."

"That is awfully suspicious, not to mention rude." His father shuts the file back in the briefcase with a click. "I should have a word with him."

Jack makes to follow his dad into the lounge, telling him, "Give him my regards," and when his father has disappeared through the door, Jack darts back inside, slipping around the dining table to get a good look at the case.

It's got a three-numbered combination lock on it. He's completely screwed.

Jack fumbles with his phone, dialing Alex's number and holding it between his ear and his shoulder.

"Hey."

Jack whispers, "Alex, real quick, how the hell do you bust into someone's combination-locked briefcase?"

"*What?*"

"Quickly!"

"Um, okay, put it upright on a table or something."

Jack does. "Check."

"Hold open the latch that opens it, now you have to listen really carefully to the mechanism, roll each of the number dials from zero until you hear a really faint click and the next dial over goes real tight."

"Okay." Jack puts the phone down on the dining table, putting his ear near the lock. He does what Alex said, holding the latch and listening for the first dial. His fingers are clumsy with urgent panic, but he hears the most delicate of clicks, feeling the middle dial go stiffer. "Six." And the next one, "four," and the final one clicks into an eight.

Alex's voice comes faintly concerned up from the table— "Jack?"—and Jack sets the dials to their correct combination.

He picks up the phone. "Done it. These things aren't very safe, are they?" He can hardly fucking breathe to whisper, but it's a hysterical kind of blabbering that he can't help. "You'd think my dad would be more careful, but he's so fucking arrogant." He carefully opens the case, finding the access ticket with Luca Baumann's signature on it stuffed under a bunch of other meaningless-looking papers. It trembles between his fingers. "Got it, we've fucking got it, Alex."

"What if he realizes it's gone?"

"He'll think he forgot it at the bank or something. It was under tons of papers."

Jack pockets the little card, slamming the case back shut. He *got it*; he's struck dumb and immobile with disbelief. All he has to do is take the file to Alex and—

His whole body freezes. There's a creak from the sitting room, loud, unmistakable, and Jack's hand lays incriminatingly flat over the lid of the briefcase.

"Jack?"

"Shh."

"Jack, *get out of there!*"

He wrenches his eyes away from the door, staggering back, twisting and throwing himself through the corner door into the kitchen. He half shuts it, hearing footsteps across the dining room floorboards, and swings open the fridge, shielding his breathless self with the fridge door.

"Man actually smelled like my vintage Glenturret," his father says haughtily, and Jack grabs a carton of orange juice, pretending to take a long drink.

He was right about Boyce, though, which is a small satisfaction.

"I was gonna make something, you want?" he asks his dad, steadily enough.

"No, I have arrangements to deal with."

"Arrangements like the first flight outta town?" Jack drawls.

His father, still with his haughty expression, aloof tone of voice, tells him, "You know I don't agree with this, Jack. I'm just taking precautions."

"I told you this will work."

"That remains to be seen."

Jack swallows, his mouth very dry. "Well, Suzanne will be here at eight-thirty, so can we at least stick around for the interview?" He has this dreadful image of rocking back up to the house later, evidence delivered, warrant pending, police poised for arrest, and his father's fled the fucking country. "You still have a campaign to win."

"First sign of trouble—"

"I know, I know, you're outta here. Just *trust* me until then, please."

His father doesn't answer yes or no, but he seems resigned all the same. He leaves Jack to the red-hot feeling of being almost caught in the act, the flood of debilitating *what if* weighing down his limbs.

He can't take much more of this. He feels like he's suffocating on lies, stuffed so full he's all clogged up with them.

Jack spends the rest of the afternoon trying to purge out his nervous energy through sketching, Alex's face a dozen aborted times and silly household items, an old glockenspiel that was a gift for his mom from some distant relative. It has a hundred intricate little patterns wound into it in gold filigree to keep him busy, but nothing dulls the sensation of time passing, the inevitable tick of the clock.

By seven-thirty, Jack's dressed and ready, pacing the sitting room.

His father comes to him, finally. Tense and quiet, radiating the kind of dread that he'd never show but that Jack feels hypersensitive to, soaking it in through his fragile skin.

"I'm sending Boyce with you."

"No, no way. If they see I have your bodyguard with me, they'll freak out."

"You don't know this isn't a trap."

"It's not," Jack snaps. He zips up his jacket for protection from the elements, his father following him out onto the porch. "I'll be back soon, you'll see."

"You're naïve if you think this will be solved by handing over a bone of contention."

Jack touches his father's shoulder.

He feels utterly human under the press of Jack's hand, warm through his cashmere. Jack tells him, "Stop being so paranoid," and lingers there, his very own Judas kiss.

"You don't know what I'm sacrificing here," his father tells him solemnly. He's less angry than Jack had expected, quietly grim as he watches his control slip away with the file in Jack's hand. Always surprising, Jack's father. "I hope you're ready to make some sacrifices of your own."

Jack's hand is left hanging in the empty air.

He watches his dad disappear inside. He watches Boyce follow blankly. The waiting car sits for Jack on the drive and a man passes him the keys.

The final hurdle, he thinks, and it's huge, horribly imposing. Everything lies at the end of this short journey; driving away from the house is just a matter of turning the key.

He navigates from the community to the highway, gate guard waving him right through, and the rain starts to fall as he turns onto Laurel Street, stop-start traffic lights blurring in the downpour and cars filled with people in suits, work uniforms, kids in the backseat—living their lives while Jack fights this one last battle for his freedom.

He pulls into the 7-Eleven lot with his heart in his mouth, and Alex's car is already sitting there idle.

Jack parks up a good distance away. He's in no doubt that Alex has seen him already, but he waits all the same, watches a woman frantically pack her groceries into her trunk under the weak cover of a flimsy umbrella. A huge black SUV pulls in, headlights cutting through the rain, and a man climbs out, running into the alley between the store and the next building over.

Jack tucks the manila folder into his zipped jacket and climbs out of the car, jogging across the asphalt to clamber into Alex's passenger seat.

It's all steamed up inside, close and muggy. The radio plays softly, some guitar number too gentle to recognize.

And Alex tells Jack, "Hey," just like he always does.

Chapter Eighteen

When he pulls back up at the house, it's starting to get dark.

The storm rages, unceasing, over his head, and he climbs the porch, noticing another car parked out front—probably Suzanne. Jack's quite late back, having taken the longest route home just to drive off some of his jitters.

And yet, he couldn't care less. He'll enthusiastically bullshit himself hoarse off right now, riding high off the exhilarating sense of imminent justice.

Alex had looked, awestruck, down at years' worth of photographs and business transactions and told Jack, "I was right, all this time and here it is."

It could be a few hours, it could be even less, and all Jack has to do is make sure his father doesn't leave this house.

Jack shakes the water out of his hair in the front hall, taking off his soaked jacket and hanging it on a hook. He listens for voices somewhere in the house and follows the faint trail of them into the lounge, heading toward the conservatory where there's a distinct breeze and the strong, metallic scent of ozone.

The back patio doors are flung open despite the weather, and the voices are coming from outside under the dry shelter of the canopy. Boyce stands watch in the doorway, stoic like always, and his father sits at the table with—definitely not Suzanne.

A man Jack's never met before, a Dictaphone laid by his hand.

"Um, hi?" Jack ventures, stepping out.

They've lit the clay chiminea, and it stands glowing warmly, burning charcoal smell heady like ancient summer nights. The garden solar lamps are all lit faintly orange, not enough light in the day to get them to full glare.

Jack can see why his father's chosen to do this outside; there's an incredible view of the rushing river from here, the lightning sporadically slicing the distant hills in two against the purplish sky.

"Jack, this is Tony," his father tells him. "He's from the Review."

Jack holds out a hand for him to shake. "What happened to Suzanne?"

"She's sick," Tony says shortly. "I'm filling in."

"O-kay." Jack takes a seat on the rickety patio furniture. He catches his father's eye. "Sorry I'm late. I, uh, had an errand to run. Went really well, though."

"That's fine, son. I was just telling Tony about the summers we used to spend in this house—you, your mother, and I."

He feels almost poignant enough to ask which ones, but he doesn't know if he has the stomach for that after what he's just done. It might be his last chance to hear those stories in his father's voice and the knowledge hurts as much as it heals.

Alex had kissed him and the sense of Jack's father's power being a permanent force felt, for the very first time, like a childish myth.

"Good times," Jack vaguely agrees.

Tony drawls, "Is that right?" He's scribbling something on a notepad, leaned back in his seat with it rested on his bent-up knee. "So, Jack, tell me about life in the campaign."

"Hectic," he answers self-deprecatingly, muscle memory taking over after all the years' practice he's had at this. "It's all about putting on a smile in the face of a difficult fight."

If he speaks in pretty soundbites, these things tend to be over fairly fast. The faster the better as far as he's concerned; Judas never had to return to look the guy he betrayed in the eye after all.

"But the reward is well worth the effort," he goes on, since nobody else seems to be talking. "My dad's a born leader. This is his calling in life."

"You encourage young voters to elect your father?" Tony asks. He seems bored, Jack dryly realizes.

"Oh, definitely." He nods. "My dad has proved himself over many elections to be the representative this district needs."

More silence; Jack looks to his father to fill it, but he's too busy staring distractedly over Jack's shoulder. Things are bad when his dad can't put on a fake smile for the public eye, bad for Jack that he seems so edgy.

Soon—so fucking soon.

"I heard," Tony belatedly reads from his paper pad, "that you got recently engaged."

"I did," Jack says flatly; it's not like he wasn't expecting this.

"How has that affected things here?"

George does step in for this one, becoming suddenly animated. "It's a parent's proudest moment, seeing their child fall in love and commit themselves to another person, but there's always some melancholy involved knowing their loyalties are going to be divided—tested, even."

Jack narrows his eyes, feeling the corner of him mouth turn up in puzzlement. Tony scribbles on his pad, hand movements all over the damn place, doesn't even look like he's writing words and somewhere behind him—Jack swears he hears the patio doors rattle like they do when someone opens the front door.

"Dad?"

"Yes, son."

He turns in his seat, looking back into the darkness of the conservatory. Were the lights on when he came through? He can't remember, mind playing tricks on him or something. "Did you hear that?"

"I didn't hear anything, Jack."

Jack turns back around, frowning. Tony's watching him intently now, his pad abandoned face-down on the table, and

Jack's skin prickles uncomfortably, meeting his eye with a sense of very real dread.

"What do you think, Jack?" he asks slyly. "Do your loyalties become strained when you fall in love?"

"I don't think I understand the question," Jack says slowly.

"It's not that difficult."

His father checks his watch, shifting to lean his elbows against the table. There's definitely a noise now, the front door slamming shut—unmistakable.

Jack blurts, "Who's in the house?" and he tries to turn, he really tries, but his father's level stare keeps him rooted. "Dad, who are you expecting?"

"A friend."

Jack jerks back, then, spinning in his seat but halted halfway by his father's vice-grip on his wrist. He drags Jack over the table, eye to eye and close enough to see that elusive madness covered by so much sophistication.

"Loyalties have to be tested, Jack," he mutters quietly. "Sometimes you have to make a true choice, not toeing the line but picking a side."

There's a for-real scuffle behind him now and Jack tears out of the grasp, kicking his chair back as if he could get any kind of distance from this situation.

Two of his father's PMCs appear out of the darkness and onto the drowsily lit patio, dragging a slumped figure between them.

Dark jeans and a leather jacket and telltale All Stars, a black bag over his head. Everything Jack has in him denies it, rejects it.

"Who—who is that?"

Boyce trails out idly after them like he hasn't a care in the damn world, kicking the figure into a kneeling position on the concrete. One look at Jack's face and he's smirking, gripping the black cloth and pulling it away with a flourish as Jack's father tells him precisely what he already knows.

"Your green-eyed boy." It sits in the throes of the thunder for a second before his father dryly adds, "Ta-da!"

Jack feels bile sting his throat. He was followed; he was watched. He kissed Alex in the parking lot and gave himself away.

Alex blinks rapidly, glancing around to get his bearings. He doesn't meet Jack's eye at all, and he's bleeding from a small wound in his hairline and—and—

"I don't understand."

That's Jack voicing his opinion there, but his voice is unrecognizable, high and childlike, and his father tells him indulgently, "I think you do, Jack," like he agrees.

Jack clears his throat; he's stronger than that, after everything. "I don't *fucking* understand. Why have you brought him here?"

"I told you, it's time to make a choice."

"What choice?" he shouts.

"Who you get into bed with, for one thing." His father walks to Alex, hunching down by his side. "I get it—sleeping with the enemy can be fun. But the time comes in a man's life when he has to stop the frivolous games and settle on his path."

"You can't be talking about yourself," Jack fires back. "I've seen what you and your buddies get up to now; you don't get to act like you're above anything."

His father contemplates this, or pretends to at least; all this talk of frivolous games and it's his father who never stops playing, never stops for a second planning move after move after countermove.

He sinks a fist into Alex's hair and drags his head back, and Jack takes a mindless step forward, grabbed by the shoulders by his farcical fake reporter as his father angles Alex's gaze toward him.

His pupils are dilated, probably from the head injury, and Jack can't do a damn thing but stare at him.

"What's your name, son?"

Alex ignores Jack's father beyond a disgusted sideways glance.

"Come on, a man shouldn't die without saying his name."

Jack chokes, "What?" and, almost theatrically, like this whole event was choreographed from his father's playbook, Tony reaches around him and presses a revolver into his hand.

Immediately, Jack tries to drop it, shake it away from him, but Tony's grip is huge and determined, sealing the weapon in Jack's closed fist.

He doesn't need to be told what's expected of him next.

"Why would I?" he mutters, first at the revolver in his hand and then at his father. "Why would I do this?"

"You'll do it or someone else will," his father says flatly.

"Him?" Jack nods toward Boyce looming over Alex from behind, then back toward Tony. "Or how about this guy? Will you make your other PMCs watch, too? Is that a part of their contract?"

"That young man is dying tonight, Jack," his father says solemnly. "Accept it and move on."

He struggles in Tony's grip, just held tighter for his trouble. "*Why*?"

"He's our enemy; he wants to bring our family down, *ruin* me. And you'd make deals with him, you'd *let* him. And why? Because he's a pretty face? A good fuck? Or is it because you're incapable of not fighting me every step of the way as I try my damndest to make you better."

"He's nobody," Jack tries desperately.

His father sneers. "He's somebody to you."

Fuck, he just doesn't have it in him to argue that. Alex looks up at him from his knees, tied and injured and so fucking beautiful it aches. Looking up at Jack like he'd forgive him if he put a bullet in him tonight just to keep his cover.

"I'm not a killer."

His father stands from his crouch. "He's probably a killer!"

Alex flinches, and Jack stares helplessly, everything there is to see right here for the bastards doing this to them.

Jack shakes his head, and his father loses it, grabbing his wrist and straightening Jack's arm with the barrel pointing downward between Alex's eyes.

"He's not walking out of here, son. It's a bullet or something far worse."

Alex's eyes flutter and skip over each of them, at the gun on him. So, so quietly, he finally speaks. "It's okay, Jack."

"Fuck you, no it isn't."

"It's *okay*."

Jack stares, horrified. His stomach clenches, bile burning the back of his throat. Staring down the metallic line of a weapon into the man he—the man he fucking *loves'* eyes, and Jack can't think of a single way out of this that doesn't involve blood on the ground.

His father lets go of him in increments, nodding to Tony to do the same, and it's the gall of it, the fucking confidence his father has that Jack can never truly get beyond his reach.

But he is so wrong. Jack's beyond it already, right here under his nose.

He thumbs the hammer back with a click, and there'll be blood on the ground, all right, but it won't be Alex's.

Jack tells him, "Don't worry," and turns and points the revolver at his father.

In a second Jack has four weapons trained on him, four voices shouting at him in no certain terms to *drop it*.

"I will pull the trigger," he warns them.

"Jack," Alex's voice tries to reason with him, but Jack shakes his head. He doesn't want to hear it.

"I should've let you die that night," Jack tell his father. He thinks he sounds a little hysterical. "You weren't worth saving."

"You're not going to shoot me, Jack."

"Let us walk out of here, and I won't have to."

"This is what you choose?" his father asks incredulously. "To die with *him*?"

"You *made* me choose!" Jack shouts, voice breaking, and the outburst riles the guards again, Boyce alone just itching to pull the trigger. "This is all on you!"

They will; there's just that sort of tension in the air, the kind that can only be cut by a bullet.

Jack's fast running out of time.

He feels it like he's outside his body, the hook of his finger bearing down on that little piece of metal. "Let us leave."

The commotion around him seems to get louder; he feels it like a crescendo. There's footsteps, boots on the ground, more men maybe, and he's going to die or he's going to pull the trigger because any minute now the decision will be out of his hands.

"Oh," is his father's reply, gaze moving past Jack's shoulder. Simple, so simply, he says, "Oh, Jack, you have been a bad boy."

Jack spins a split-second before the shadow barrels into him and all fucking hell breaks loose.

The sound of boots is tremendous, of weapons cocking, of people shouting; it's a senseless cacophony, and Jack's spooked like a startled animal, struggling violently to get up, get the body off him.

"Saint, get over here and deal with your guy."

He sees nothing but dark bodies moving until his wrist is gripped, and he's pulled away.

"George Preston, you are under arrest on suspicion of fraud, embezzlement, the bribery of public officials—"

Alex's face comes into focus against the smoky remains of the chiminea; Jack feels like he's hit his head, the world taking its sweet-ass time to right itself, the periphery view of his father getting cuffed like a vision from a dream that can't possibly be true when just a second ago—

Alex keeps his hold around Jack's wrist, and they watch, jointly, as Jack's father is manhandled

It's real, all right, anchored by Alex's trembling hand on him. Real and undeniable, and Jack still can't believe it.

But he watches—he *watches* his father being led away, surrounded by cops, some kind of SWAT team by the looks of it, with his face hollowed by the same kind of shock, the exact disbelief.

"Do you wanna—" Alex starts, but Jack's already moving, striding forward while Alex waves away the concern of the armed escorts.

Jack's father stares with wide eyes in the mouth of the patio door, and Jack towers over him, feels bigger than him in every way. *"Ta-da."*

"Not bad, son," he gets out through his gritted teeth.

"I wonder," Jack says softly, still too overwhelmed to make his voice steady, "how you'll cope without your freedom."

"It'll only be a matter of time before I'm out."

"Oh, no." Jack shakes his head. "You're never getting out, *trust* me."

And with that, with his father's face collapsing to ruin, Alex's hand curling around Jack's wrist, his dad is gone, hauled off through the house, shouting curses, struggling against people far stronger than him.

Jack listens to the echoes of it. He'll never hear that voice again in this place, in any place that means something.

"C'mon," Alex mutters close to his ear. "There's nothing left to see here."

They walk through the milling cops like two ghosts, like Alex really is effective armor against regular procedure.

The front porch is slippery with rainwater, almost too difficult for Jack's numb body to navigate. There's wailing cop cars everywhere on the drive, the whole place lit up like the fourth of July, and the lights flash epileptically through the rain, making his vision swim.

Alex ducks him through the storm and into the passenger seat of a car, crouching by the open door.

"They're gonna want to interview you."

Jack rubs at his face. "Yeah, okay."

Alex studies him for a second, telling him, "Wait here," and disappears into the throng of bodies.

Question him. About his father. About his involvement in the operation. About Alex and their lies and their extremely recent brush with death.

But only Alex jogs back to him, appearing through the deluge like a curtain drawn back, and Jack stands and lets himself get doused, soaked to his skin.

Alex raises his voice over the white noise of it all, blinking water out of his eyes. "What are you doing?"

"Where is he?" Jack demands, reaching out to grip both Alex's hands in his own.

"On his way to the station already." Alex squints at him. "Jack?"

He takes great staggering gulps of breath through his open mouth, tipping his head down to let the rain run off the ends of his hair.

"Jack!"

It's shocking like a slap, and Jack's hold is shaken to make way for Alex's hands cupping his face.

"It's over," Jack chokes out, and again, "It's over," until Alex nods, expression awestruck.

"Yeah, it's over."

Jack presses forward clumsily, kissing the rainwater from his mouth. His arms slip all the way around Alex's middle, pulling his arching body up damp and close everywhere.

Alex breathes against the corner of Jack's mouth. "Let's get away from this place."

"Interview?"

"It can wait for now."

He dealt with it, still protecting Jack even now, and Jack honestly didn't expect any different, the strength of trust almost too huge to bear.

"Then I wanna go home. My home."

"Okay." Alex nudges his nose against Jack's. "Let me take you home."

Epilogue

And so home is where Alex takes him, the familiar route through the city all the way south.

Seeing his building is like a gut-punch, sandblasted and old as the city herself, beaten by the relentless rain, and Jack tips his head back against the seat and laughs.

Alex asks, "What?" and Jack shakes his head.

"Suddenly I don't wanna go inside."

"How come?"

"It's like—like walking back into an old high school when you've aged a decade," he huffs. "You can't go back."

There's a thoughtful silence, and then Alex says softly, "I'll come up with you. Chase off the ghosts."

Jack grins at him, swollen with it.

He doesn't know what he's going to find in there, but it won't be the same as what he left, with or without Alex by his side. Nothing will be the same and maybe—maybe Jack's okay with that after all, the sense of *same* a redundant concept anyway when his life so far has been ruled with an iron fist both with and without his knowledge.

"Saint," Jack remembers suddenly. "Some guy called you Saint."

"Alex Saint."

Jack marvels at him. "Wanna come up to my apartment, Alex Saint, man now of little-to-no mystery?"

"Gladly."

His place is just another reminder, but it's time to face it like he has everything else so far, put those ghosts to rest one by one.

And Alex *is* by his side, full name and all, and that's enough to hope for a different kind of future.

About the Author

Elizabeth is a debut author from the north of England. With a long-time passion for writing, at eight years old she attempted to write and illustrated her very own Goosebumps books, as well as an ongoing series of solve-it-yourself mysteries, and several stories about a single lady living her life with an unfortunate perm. One day she hopes that practice will pay off, but until then she's been recently adopted by two cats and gets by working for the government.

Email: libbydwilde@hotmail.com

Website: https://elizabethdwilde.wordpress.com/

Twitter: twitter.com/elizabethdwilde

NineStar Press, LLC

www.ninestarpress.com

www.ingramcontent.com/pod-product-compliance
Lightning Source LLC
Chambersburg PA
CBHW050715180626
46814CB00002B/443